The Life of a Good-for-nothing

JOSEPH, FREIHERR VON EICHENDORFF was born in Silesia in 1788. He studied law at Halle and Heidelberg, and then lived in Vienna until 1813, when he joined the Prussian army. In 1816 he was appointed to a judicial office at Breslau, and this appointment was followed by similar ones at Danzig, Konigsberg and Berlin. He died at Neisse in 1857.

Eichendorff is best known for his lyric poetry, and is one of the finest poets of the later German romantic school. Many of his poems, celebrating the moods of nature and the life of the wanderer, have been set to music by Schubert. He also wrote plays and short romances, and of these *Aus dem Leben eines Taugenichts*, which appeared in 1826, is the most famous.

THE LIFE OF A
GOOD-FOR-NOTHING

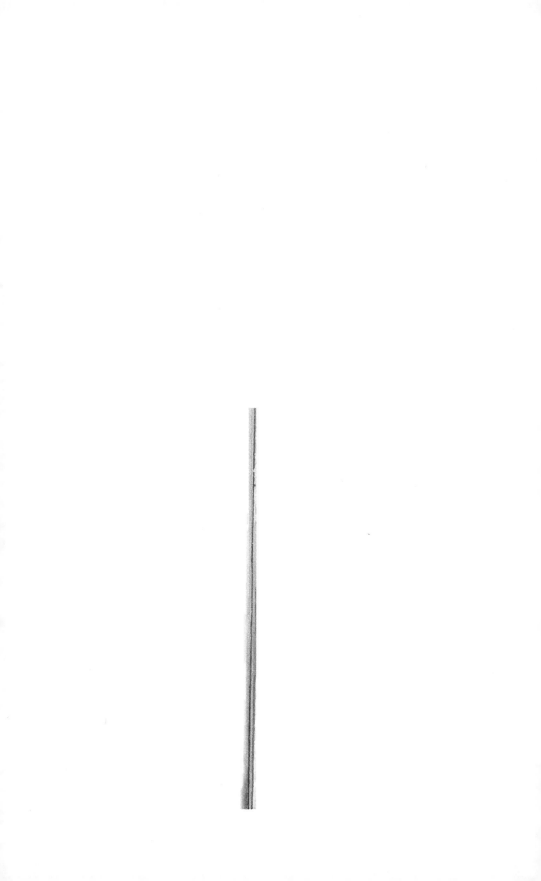

THE LIFE OF A
GOOD-FOR-NOTHING

JOSEPH, FREIHERR von EICHENDORFF

TRANSLATED FROM THE GERMAN BY MICHAEL GLENNY

BLACKIE

LONDON & GLASGOW

Blackie & Son Ltd., 5 Fitzhardinge Street, London, W.1
Bishopbriggs, Glasgow
Blackie & Son (India) Ltd., Bombay
Printed in Great Britain by Blackie & Son Ltd., Glasgow

THE LIFE OF A
GOOD-FOR-NOTHING

—◦૪-૭®ᐟᐠᐟᐟᐧᐧᐧᐧ₢ᐟᐧᐧᐧ₢-૪◦—

Once more the wheel of my father's mill was humming and gurgling right merrily, the snow was dripping busily from the roof and the sparrows twittering and bustling back and forth as I sat upon the threshold and rubbed the sleep from my eyes; I loved to be in the warm sunshine. Then my father stepped out of the house; since daybreak he had been a-rummaging in the mill, his nightcap askew on his head. Said he to me: 'You good-for-nothing! There you sit sunning yourself, lolling and stretching your limbs to exhaustion and leaving me to do all the work alone. I can feed you here no longer. Spring's at the gate, go out into the world and earn your own bread for once in your life.'

'Well,' said I, 'if I am a good-for-nothing, so be it; I will set out and make my fortune.' Indeed I was glad to go, for I had lately been thinking of setting off on my travels; I could hear how the yellow-hammer, who all autumn and winter had piped sadly at our window—'Farmer, *hire* me, Farmer, *hire* me'—now in the sweet springtime had proudly changed his tune to a gay 'Farmer can *keep* his work!'

So I went indoors and took down my fiddle, which I played well enough. My father gave me a few groats for the road and I sauntered down the long village street and away. To my secret joy I saw all my old friends and comrades going out to work, to dig and plough as they had done yesterday and the day before and would do forever, while I strolled out so free into the wide world. Proud and happy I called adieu right and left to the poor people, but not one of them paid me heed. It was as if life were an endless Sunday, and when at last I reached the open fields I put up my beloved fiddle and played and sang as I went along:

The man elect to God's salvation
Moves in a world where wonders teem,
Is shown the wonders of creation
In mountain, wood, in field and stream.

Slow spirits by their firesides lying
Are never quickened by the morn,
They understand an infant crying,
And care and need and hope forlorn.

Streams gush and babble down the mountain,
A lark rides on the shining air,
I, too, must sing with lark and fountain,
Full-throated, fresh and free of care.

God's ways and works charm and content me,
His streams, his larks, his heaven, his earth:
Each field and wood in which he sent me
Has brought me joy and blessed my birth.

As I looked about me there drew near to me an elegant travelling coach, which must have been driving along behind me for some time without my perceiving it, so full was my heart with music; for it was driving quite slowly and two fine ladies were stretching their heads out of the coach and listening to me. One of them was especially beautiful and younger than the other, but in truth I liked both of them. As I stopped singing the elder of the two ordered the coach to halt and said graciously to me: 'Now there's a merry lad who can sing a pretty song.' To which I answered smartly: 'If it were to oblige your grace I could sing some much sweeter.' Whereat she questioned me further: 'And where might he be going so early this fine morning?' I was ashamed, not knowing myself whither I was bound, but said boldly: 'To Vienna.' They then spoke to each other in a strange language which I did not understand. The younger of them shook her head several times, but the other only laughed and laughed and finally called to me: 'Jump up behind, we are going to Vienna.' What an invitation! I made a bow and was up behind the coach in one leap, the coachman cracked his whip and we flew off along the shining road at a pace that made the wind whistle round my hat.

Village, garden and church tower now faded behind me as new villages, castles and mountains appeared ahead; standing corn, bushes and meadows flew gaily by, countless larks sang in the clear blue air. I was too shy to shout aloud, but inwardly I rejoiced and stamped and danced about so much on the running-board that I soon almost lost my fiddle which I was holding under my arm. But as the sun climbed higher and higher, the heavy white midday clouds rose up round the horizon; as everything in the air and on the broad plain grew empty and a sultry calm settled over the gently waving cornfields, only then did I remember my village, my father and our mill, how

3

still and cool it had been by the shady mill-pool and how far, far behind me it now all lay. I had a curious feeling, as though I must turn back; I stuck my fiddle between jacket and waistcoat, sat down pensively on the running-board and fell asleep.

When I opened my eyes the coach had stopped under some tall lime trees, beyond which broad steps led between columns up to a stately castle. Beyond, I saw the towers of Vienna through the trees. The ladies, it seemed, had long since alighted and the horses had been unharnessed. Sitting there all alone I took fright and as I ran into the house I heard laughter from a window.

I was wonderfully pleased to be in this great palace. As I cast my first looks around in the cool, spacious entrance hall, someone tapped me on the shoulder with a stick. I turned round and there stood a tall gentleman in livery, a broad sash of silk and gold hanging down to his waist, a silver-topped staff in his hand and an unusually long, curved imperial nose on his face, as grand as a puffed-up turkey-cock, who asked me who I was and what I wanted here. I was dumbfounded and speechless with fear and amazement. At that moment a host of servants came running from above and below stairs, saying nothing, but looking me up and down from top to toe. Then a chamber-maid (as I later learned she was) came straight up to me and said that I was a charming boy and that her gracious mistress wished to know if I cared to serve her as a gardener's lad. I clutched my waistcoat; my few groats must, I suppose, have been flung out of their pocket by the jolting of the coach and were gone. I had nothing but my fiddle for which, the gentleman with the staff had said as he walked by, he would not give me a penny. In my anguish at this I said to the chambermaid, 'Yes,' still gazing sideways at the menacing figure who continued to pace up and down the hallway like the pendulum of a church clock and who was just approaching again from the further part of the hall with awful and majestic tread. Finally the gardener appeared, muttered into his beard something about vagabonds and peasant bumpkins and led me to the garden, subjecting me to a lengthy homily on the way: how I was always to be sober and industrious, not to wander abroad, not to waste time on unprofitable and useless occupations and how I might then, with time, come to some good. There were many more fair, well-phrased and useful precepts, but I have meanwhile as good as forgotten them all. I was still not entirely sure what had happened to me, but merely answered Yes to it all, for I felt like a bird whose wings had been doused. At least, thank God, I was assured of my bread and butter.

Life in the garden was pleasant. I had my daily fill of hot food and more money than I needed for wine, only unfortunately I also had rather much to do. I delighted in the temples, bowers and fair green alleyways and would have loved them more had I but been allowed to walk round them at my ease and in sensible discourse as did the gentlemen and ladies who daily visited the garden. Whenever the gardener was away and I was alone, I would at once take out my short pipe, sit down and imagine all the polite turns of speech which I should address, were I her suitor, to the beautiful young lady

5

who had brought me here. Or on sultry afternoons I would lie on my back, when everything was so quiet that the only sound was the humming of the bees, and watch the clouds above me flying towards my village, the grasses and flowers swaying to and fro; as I thought of that lady it would often happen that the fair creature would pass through the garden in the distance, a guitar or a book in her hand, so quiet, so angelically charming that I was not sure whether I was dreaming or waking.

One day, as I was passing a summer-house on my way to work, I was singing this song to myself:

> Where'ere my roaming finds me,
> Where mountain skies are blue,
> Your beauty, lady, blinds me,
> Each field and wood reminds me
> A thousand times of you

Just then I saw two sweet, young, fresh eyes sparkling forth from the cool dark summer-house between the half-open shutters and the flowers that stood behind them. I was so frightened that I did not finish my song but went on to my work without looking around me.

One evening—it was a Saturday and I was already enjoying the coming Sunday in anticipation—I was standing at the window of the gardener's lodge with my fiddle and still thinking of those sparkling eyes, when suddenly the chambermaid came slipping through the twilight. 'My lady sends you something with which you may drink her health—and she wishes you a good night!' With that she smartly set a bottle of wine on my window-sill and vanished through the flowerbeds and hedges like a little lizard.

6

I stood for a long time in front of that wonderful bottle, unable to grasp my good fortune. Where once I had scraped my fiddle merrily enough, now I played and sang with a will; I sang the song of the fair lady to its end and all the other songs that I knew, until the nightingales were out and moon and stars had long risen over the garden. What a night that was!

None of us knows in our cradle what will become of him, even a blind hen will often find a grain, he laughs best who laughs last, the unexpected often happens, man proposes and God disposes—thus I meditated as I again sat in the garden with my pipe next day and I almost felt, so carefully did I examine myself, that I had been moonstruck. I had now taken to getting up very early every day, quite contrary to my usual habit, before the gardener and the other workmen were stirring. It was so beautiful out in the garden at that hour. The flowers, the fountains, the rosebushes, the whole garden sparkled in the morning sun like pure gold and precious stones. In the tall avenues of beeches it was as still, as cool and as solemn as in a church, except for the birds that fluttered and pecked at the soil. Before the great house, below the very window where the fair lady lived, was a flowering shrub. There I would go very early every morning and crouch beneath its branches in order to gaze at her windows, for I had not the valour to show myself in the open. There I would always see my beauty come to the window, still warm and half asleep in a snow-white gown. Now she would begin to plait her dark brown hair while her playful gaze would wander over bush and garden, now she would bend down and gather the

7

flowers which grew under her window, or she would lay her guitar in her white arm and sing out over the garden so wonderfully that my heart still leaps even now when I recall one of those songs—but oh, that is all so long ago!

This lasted a week or more, but one day when she was again standing at the window and all around was still, a fatal fly buzzed into my nose and I gave such a fearful sneeze that I could not stop. She leaned far out of the window and saw me, oh horror, lurking in the bush. I was so ashamed that I did not come back for several days.

Finally I plucked up courage and went again, but this time the window was shut; four, five, six mornings I sat behind the shrub but she did not appear again at the window. Then I grew impatient and with great boldness I walked openly up and down past all the windows of the great house, but my dear lady still stayed away. A little further along, however, I always saw the other lady standing at the window. I had never before looked at her so closely. She was in truth also something of a beauty, plump and pink, full-blown and proud in appearance like a tulip. I always made her a deep bow and I must admit that she thanked me every time, nodded and lowered her eyes most politely in response. Once only I thought that I saw my beauty herself standing at the window behind the curtain and peeping out from her hiding-place.

Many days went by, however, without my seeing her. She no longer came into the garden or to her window. The gardener called me a lazy oaf, I was peevish and the tip of my own nose seemed to be in my way whenever I stared out at the world.

One Sunday afternoon I lay in the garden and as I stared through the blue tobacco-clouds from my pipe I reproached myself for not having taken up some other work in which I would at least have had a Monday half-holiday to look forward to. Meanwhile the other lads had probably all gone, decked out in their best, to the dance halls in the nearby outskirts of the city. There, in the warm breeze, they would all be strolling and weaving their excited way in their Sunday finery between the brightly lit houses and the wandering barrel-organs. Yet I squatted in the reeds of a remote pond in the garden, like that solitary bird the bittern, rocking myself in the punt moored to the bank, while the vesper bells of the city echoed over the garden and the swans paddled slowly to and fro beside me on the water. I was in deathly anguish.

Just then I heard a babble of distant voices, of gay chatter and laughter coming nearer and nearer, soon there came flashes of red and white scarves, hats and plumes through the greenery and all at once a bright crowd of young ladies and gentlemen from the castle came across the meadow and were upon me, among them my two ladies. I stood up and was about to go, when the elder of the two fair ladies espied me. 'Aha, well met!' she cried with a smile. 'He can row us over the pond to the far side.' One after the other, with caution and trepidation, the ladies now embarked on the punt, the gentlemen helping them and showing not a little pride at their boldness on the water. When all the ladies were seated on the thwarts,

I pushed off from the bank. One of the young gentlemen standing up in the bow began imperceptibly to rock the craft, at which the ladies turned hither and thither in fright and some cried out. My beauty sat with a lily in her hand close by the little boat's side and, smiling to herself, gazed down into the clear waves; as she touched them with the lily her image was repeated in the water between the reflections of clouds and trees, like an angel gently floating through the deep blue of the heavenly vault.

As I gazed at her thus, the cheerful, plump one of my two ladies suddenly decided that I should sing to them as we sailed along. At that a very elegant young gentleman, with a pair of spectacles on his nose, who was seated beside her, quickly turned towards her, softly kissed her hand and said: 'Oh, thank you for that charming thought! A folk song, sung by one of the people in the freedom of the woods and fields is like an alpine rose growing wild on the mountainside—your collections of so-called folk songs are nothing but picture-book flowers by comparison—it is the very heart and soul of our people.' I said, though, that I knew of nothing to sing which was good enough for such fine company. Then the pert little chambermaid, who was standing close beside me with a basket full of cups and bottles and whom until then I had not noticed at all, said: 'But he knows a very pretty song about a beautiful lady.' 'Yes, yes, he must sing that song as boldly as only he can,' answered the lady at once. I blushed more and more. At that my beauty looked up from the water and gave me a look which pierced me body and soul. I thought no more, seized my courage and sang with a full-chested vigour:

Where'ere my roaming finds me,
Where mountain skies are blue,
Your beauty, lady, blinds me,
Each field and wood reminds me
A thousand times of you.

My garden flowers I take for
A garland fresh and fair,
A garland I might make for,
The thousand thoughts which ache for
The greeting I would bear.

She never could receive them,
She is too fine and pure,
They fade e'en as I weave them,
So in my heart I leave them
Where love must still endure.

My joy might seem unending,
My work is brisk and brave,
While to my flowers bending,
My broken heart's not mending:
I'll soon have dug my grave.

We touched land, the company disembarked; I had not
failed to notice that while I sang several of the young
gentlemen had mocked me to the ladies with sly glances
and whispers. As he went, the gentleman in the spectacles
clasped me by the hand and said something to me—what
it was I cannot even remember—and the elder of my two
ladies gave me a very kind look. Throughout my song my
beauty herself had sat with downcast eyes and had gone
away, saying nothing. But even as I sang tears were in my
eyes, my heart nearly broke with pain and shame at my
song and only now did I see how truly beautiful she was

and how poor, despised and abandoned was I. When they had disappeared through the bushes I could contain my feelings no longer, but threw myself down on the grass and wept bitterly.

2

The road ran alongside the estate, only separated from the garden by a high wall. Beside it stood a neat little toll-house with a red tiled roof and a gaily-fenced flower garden; a hole in the wall led from it to the shadiest and most secluded part of the castle garden. The toll-keeper who occupied it had recently died. One morning early when I was still fast asleep, the clerk of the estate came to me and roused me to go at once to the bailiff. I quickly dressed and ambled off behind the jolly clerk, who as he went broke off a flower, now here, now there, and stuck it in his button-hole, now made a few mock fencing-passes in the air with his walking stick and chattered endlessly to me—of which I grasped nothing, as my eyes and ears were still full of sleep. As I entered the estate office, it being still before daybreak, the bailiff looked at me from behind an enormous inkwell and piles of books and papers; staring from beneath a handsome peruke like an owl from its nest he addressed me: 'What might your name be? Whence do you come? Can you write, read and reckon?' Receiving my affirmative answer he went on: 'Well, my lad, their gracious lordships, having regard to your good conduct and particular merits, have proposed you for the vacant post of toll-keeper.' I took momentary stock of my previous behaviour and manners and having done so I was obliged to admit that the bailiff was right and before I had time to turn round I became a toll-keeper.

I at once took over my new dwelling and was soon settled in. I found many implements which the late toll-keeper had bequeathed to his successor, among them a gorgeous red dressing gown with yellow dots, a nightcap and several long-stemmed pipes. In my days at home I had longed to possess all these, having seen our vicar parading with such complacency in like array. The whole day long (for I had nothing else to do) I sat in dressing gown and nightcap on the little bench in front of my house, smoked the longest-stemmed of the pipes which I had inherited from my sainted predecessor and watched the people as they walked, drove or rode up and down the turnpike. My only wish was that once in a while a few of the folk from my own village, who had always said I would never come to anything in all my days, might pass by and see me. The dressing gown admirably suited my looks and I was thoroughly pleased with my situation. There I sat and pondered on this and that—how all beginnings are difficult and what comforts there were in a life of respectability; I secretly resolved to give up travelling, even to save money as others did and with time to make my way to some position in the world. Meanwhile, though, I forgot nothing of my resolves, cares and stratagems regarding my fair one. I threw out the potatoes and other vegetables which I found growing in my little garden and planted it entirely with the choicest flowers, at which the castle porter, he of the imperial nose, who often visited me since my move into the toll-booth and had become my intimate friend, looked at me askance and considered me to be one of those whom sudden fortune robs of their senses. But I paid no heed, for in the nearby castle garden I could hear the sound of gentle voices, among which I felt sure I recognized that of my beauteous lady, despite the thickets which hid them from my view. Every day I tied up a bouquet of the prettiest flowers that I had, climbed over the wall every evening after dark and laid them on a stone table which stood in an arbour; every evening when I brought a fresh bunch the other was gone from the table.

One evening the gentry had ridden out hunting; the sun was about to set, bathing the countryside in a shining glow, the Danube rippled away in the distance as though made of pure gold and fire, while from every hillside into the furthest distance echoed the joyous song of the vine-dressers. I was sitting with the porter on the bench in front of my house and enjoying the spectacle of that happy day slowly darkening and declining in the warm air. Suddenly the horns of the returning hunters were heard in the distance, echoing back and forth from the hills opposite. My inmost heart was touched and I sprang up and cried as if bewitched: 'Ah, that is the life for me, the noble sport of hunting!'

The porter, however, calmly knocked out his pipe and said: 'So you may think, but I have taken part in it; they hardly pay you enough to replace the shoe-leather which you wear out and you never throw off the coughs and sneezes you catch from wet feet.' For some reason a foolish anger seized me with such strength that my whole body trembled. Suddenly I found the fellow and everything about him repellent, his dull coat, his perpetual complaints about his feet, his snuff and his big nose. As though beside myself I seized him by the chest and said: 'Porter—be off home with you or I will thrash you on the spot!' At these words the porter reverted to his former view of me, namely that I was demented. He stared at me with suspicion and trepidation, made off without a word and, with many a backward scowl, strode away to the castle, where he breathlessly described how I was now turned raving mad.

I could not but laugh with delight at being rid of that know-all, for the time had nearly come at which I was wont to put my bunch of flowers in the arbour. Today, too, I leaped smartly over the wall and was just approaching the little stone table when I heard the sound of nearby horse's hooves. There was no time to run away, for my gracious lady herself was riding slowly towards me down the avenue, dressed in green hunting habit and plumed hat. She seemed to be deep in thought. My feelings were exactly those which had once seized me when, at home with my father, I had read in old books of the fair Magelone and how she had advanced through the tall trees to the ever-approaching sound of hunting horns and the glancing lights of evening—I could not move from the spot. She took fright as she suddenly became aware of me and halted almost as if against her will. My heart pounding with joy, I was as though stupefied with anxiety, and when I noticed that she was in truth wearing my bouquet of yesterday at her breast I could contain myself no longer but said in great confusion: 'Most gracious, fairest

16

lady, take this bouquet too, from me, take all the flowers from my garden and everything that I have. Ah, were there but need I would go through fire for you!' At first she gazed at me with a look of such earnestness, indeed almost of anger, that I was stricken to the marrow of my bones, and her eyes remained deeply downcast for as long as I spoke. Just then the sound of riders' voices was heard from the bushes; she quickly took the bunch from my hand and, without saying a word, she had vanished round the corner of the avenue in a moment. From that evening on I had no more peace. In mood I was perpetually as I am prone to feel on the threshold of spring, joyous yet uneasy without knowing why, as though a great happiness or some other prodigious event were awaiting me. In particular the art of calculating, at which I never excelled, now began to elude me altogether and whenever the sunshine fell golden-green through the leaves of the chestnut tree outside my window on to my figures and played tricks between 'Carried Forward' and 'Brought Forward', I had such strange thoughts that I often grew quite fuddled and truly incapable of counting up to three. Then the figure 'eight' would begin to look like the tightly laced lady with a broad cap, the evil 'seven' like a backward-pointing signpost or a gallows. The jolliest figure was the 'nine' which would always stand on its head and turn into a 'six' when I was not looking, whilst the 'two' looked so quizzically like a question-mark as if it were saying to me: 'And what is to become of you, you poor "nought"? Without *her*, that slim figure "one", you will never amount to anything!' I no longer even enjoyed sitting out of doors. To be more comfortable I took a stool with me and stretched my feet upon it. I patched an old parasol that had belonged to the toll-keeper and opened it over me against the sun like a Chinese pagoda. But none of this helped. It seemed to me as I sat there and smoked and speculated as though my legs were growing slowly longer from boredom and my nose were gradually being stretched out from so many hours of staring at it. And on the many occasions, often before daybreak, when a special mail-coach came by and I walked out half asleep into the cool air and a charming little face, whose sparkling eyes were the only features that could be descried in the half-light, would lean with curiosity from the coach and bid me a friendly good morning; when the cocks in the surrounding villages crowed so sharply over the gently waving cornfields, a few early-risen larks were scudding high in the sky between the swathes of morning mist and the postilion would pick up his post-horn and drive on blowing and blowing—then I would stand long and watch the coach disappear and feel that I must at once take to the road myself and be off into the wide wide world.

Meanwhile I still continued, as soon as the sun set, to lay my bouquets on the stone table in the dark arbour, but to tell the truth it had been a failure since that evening: they were now disregarded. Whenever I looked early in the morning, the flowers lay there as on the day before and looked at me sadly with their wilted, drooping little heads and drops of dew like tears. This grieved me deeply. I made up no more bouquets. From now onward the weeds might grow in my garden as they wished and I let the flowers stand there and grow until the wind blew their petals away and my heart felt as wild, as neglected as those flowers.

It was at this critical time then, that one day as I lay at home by the window staring gloomily out into the empty air, the chambermaid from the castle came tripping across the road. As soon as she caught sight of me she turned towards me and stopped at the window. 'The master returned yesterday from his travels,' she said quickly. 'Indeed?' I countered in astonishment—I had paid so little heed to events for several weeks that I was not even aware that the master had been away—'Then his daughter, my gracious lady, will be delighted.' The chambermaid looked me up and down so curiously that I was obliged to wonder whether I had said anything stupid. 'Oh, but you know nothing,' said she finally, wrinkling her little nose. 'Now,' she went on, 'tonight there will be a ball and masquerade at the castle in the master's honour. My lady too will be masked and costumed as a gardener—do you understand me?—as a gardener. Now my lady has seen that the flowers in your garden are especially pretty.'

That is strange, I thought to myself, since there are now hardly any flowers to be seen in it for weeds. But she continued: 'Since my lady needs flowers to go with her costume, freshly picked flowers, you are to bring her some and to wait with them after dark under the big pear tree in the castle garden; there she will come and fetch her flowers.'

I was quite speechless with joy at this news and in my delight I leaped out of the window at the chambermaid.

'O fie, what a horrible old dressing gown!' she cried. as she suddenly saw how I was dressed. This vexed me, but not wanting to be backward in gallantry I made a few skips and lunges to clasp her and kiss her. Unfortunately as I did so my dressing gown, which was far too long for me, became tangled in my feet and I measured my length on the ground. By the time that I had picked myself up the chambermaid was off and away and I could hear her in the distance laughing so hard that she had to hold her sides.

Now I had some pleasing food for thought. She had remembered me and my flowers! I went into my garden, hastily pulled all the weeds from the beds and threw them over my head into the bright sky as though by pulling them out I was uprooting all evil and melancholy. Now the roses were like her mouth again, the sky-blue convolvulus were like her eyes and the snow-white lily with its head bowed in melancholy was the very image of her. I laid them all carefully in a basket. It was a beautiful still evening with not a trace of cloud in the sky. A few stars had already risen in the firmament, far away the Danube whispered past the meadows and near by countless birds sang lustily in the great trees of the master's garden. Oh, I was so happy! When at last night fell I took my basket on my arm and set off for the big garden. The basket was so full of charm and colour, white, red, blue and scented, that my heart danced at the very sight.

Full of merry thoughts I walked in the beautiful moonlight along the quiet, neatly sanded paths, over the little white bridges beneath which the swans slept on the water and passed the delicate bowers and summer-houses. I soon reached the big pear tree, for it was the same one under which I had lain on sultry afternoons as a gardener's boy.

It was dark and lonely here. Only the silver leaves of an aspen trembled and whispered without cease. Snatches of dance music occasionally echoed from the castle and now and again I could hear voices in the garden which often came quite near, only to be followed by complete stillness.

My heart was beating. I thrilled with a strange feeling, as though I were about to commit robbery. For a long time I stood leaning stock-still against the tree and listened all around me, but still no one came and I could endure it no longer. I hooked my basket over my arm and quickly climbed up into the pear tree in order to be in the free fresh air again.

Once up there the dance music could clearly be heard over the tree-tops. I could see over the whole garden and right into the brightly lit windows of the castle. There the chandeliers were turning slowly like garlands of stars; as in a shadow play countless elegant lords and their ladies wove and waltzed and criss-crossed in gay confusion, whilst now and again some would lean out of the window and look down into the garden. Outside the castle the lawns, the shrubs and trees stood as if gilded by the multitude of lights from the ballroom, in which the flowers and birds seemed to have awakened into life. Further away, all around and behind me the rest of the garden lay black and still. There she is, dancing away, I thought to myself up there in the tree, and has certainly long ago forgotten you and your flowers. They are all so gay, not a soul has a thought for you. And that is my fate, always and everywhere. Everyone has his own little spot on earth, his own warm stove, his cup of coffee, his wife, his glass of wine of an evening and he is truly happy withal; even that great long stick of a porter is content with his life. I belong nowhere: it is as if I arrived everywhere too late, as though the whole world had simply failed to reckon with my existence.

As I philosophized thus I suddenly heard something come rustling towards me in the grass. Two gentle voices were quietly talking somewhere near by. After a few moments the branches of the shrubs were parted and the chambermaid's little face appeared through the branches as she looked all around her. The moonlight sparkled in her mischievous eyes as she stared out. It was not long before the lady dressed as a gardener also stepped out between the trees, looking just as the chambermaid had described her to me yesterday. My heart beat as if to burst. She was wearing a mask and gazed around her in surprise, at which it suddenly seemed to me that she was not quite so slim and delicate after all: finally she stepped close to the tree and took off her mask—in truth it was not my young beauty but the other, the elder!

How glad I now was, when I had recovered from my first shock, that I was sitting up here in safety. How in heaven's name, thought I, does *this* one come to be here? If my dear young one comes now to fetch her flowers— what a scene there will be! I could have wept with vexation at the whole spectacle.

Meanwhile below me the disguised gardener spoke up: 'It is so stiflingly hot there in the ballroom that I was simply obliged to take a walk and to cool off a little out in the sweet fresh air.' So saying she fanned herself unceasingly with her mask and puffed away. In the bright moonlight I could clearly see how the tendons in her neck were puffed and swollen; she looked brick-red and angry. The chambermaid continued to search behind every bush as though she had lost a needle.

'I so badly need some fresh flowers to go with my mask,' went on the false gardener, 'where can he be?' The chambermaid searched on, giggling to herself all the while. 'Did you say something, Rosette?' asked the lady sharply. 'I was saying what I have always said,' replied the chambermaid, putting on an honest and serious face, 'that our young toll-keeper is nothing but an idle bump-kin and is sure to be lying somewhere asleep behind a bush.' This made me twitch in every limb and want to jump down and defend my reputation, when suddenly a great sound of music and kettledrums was heard from the castle.

The gardener's lass could contain herself no longer. 'Oh, now they are going to give a cheer for my lord,' she snapped. 'Come, we shall be missed.' With this she quickly donned her mask and set off in a fury to return with the chambermaid to the castle. The trees and bushes seemed to point inquisitively after her, as if with long fingers and sharp noses, the moonlight played up and down her broad waist as though over a keyboard and so she made her exit to the sound of drums and trumpets, for all the world like an opera singer leaving the stage.

Up there in my tree I was ignorant of what had happened and I now fixed my gaze on the castle, where a circle of torches on the lower steps of the entrance was throwing a strange glow over the glittering windows and far out into the garden. It was the servants, who were serenading their young mistress. In the midst of them

23

stood the porter as magnificently bedizened as a minister of state, puffing industriously at a bassoon in front of a music-stand. As I was settling myself comfortably to listen to the beautiful serenade, the double doors on the castle balcony suddenly opened. A noble gentleman, handsome and stately in his uniform adorned with many glittering stars, stepped out on to the balcony, holding by the hand my gracious young lady in a pure white dress, looking like a lily in the light of the moon rising over the clear firmament.

I could not turn my eyes from that spot. Garden, trees and meadows vanished from my senses as she stood there, tall and slim, wonderfully lit by the torches as she turned gracefully, now to speak to the handsome officer, now to give a friendly nod to the musicians below. The people below were beside themselves with joy and finally I could no longer restrain myself either and joined in the shouts of Hurrah! with all the force in my body.

But when soon afterwards she disappeared from the balcony, the torches below were extinguished one by one, the music-stands were removed and the garden round about grew dark again and its rustling sounds were heard as before—only then did I realize, only then was my heart aware that no one but the aunt had summoned me to supply her with flowers, that my fair one was long since married and had forgotten me and I was nothing but a great fool.

All this plunged me into an abyss of meditation. I curled up like a hedgehog within the prickly spines of my own thoughts. The dance music from the castle could now be heard less often, solitary clouds floated away over the dark garden. And there I sat up in my tree like an owl in the ruins of my happiness the whole night through.

The cool morning air finally wakened me from my reverie. I was thoroughly astonished when I looked around. The music and dancing had long since ceased; everything in and around the castle, on the lawns, on the stone steps and between the columns looked so still, so cool and solemn; only the fountain before the entrance played its lonely tune as it splashed away. Here and there in the branches beside me the birds were already waking; they shook their bright feathers and as they stretched their little wings they stared with surprise and curiosity at their strange bedfellow. The rays of the morning sun flickered gaily at me and flashed over the garden.

I stood up in the tree and for the first time in a long while I could see far over the countryside, to where a few barges were already sailing down the Danube between the vineyards and where the still empty highroads swung out like bridges over the shining landscape towards distant hill and dale. I do not know how it came, but all at once I was seized by all my old longing to travel, all the old joy, the yearning and the high expectation. At the same moment I thought how my beauty was sleeping up there in the castle among flowers and between silken sheets with an angel sitting on her bed in the still of the morning. 'No,' I cried, 'I must away from here, away to as far as the sky is blue!'

At that I picked up my basket and threw it high into the air, scattering the poor flowers so that they fell through the branches and lay like so many specks of colour on the grass beneath. Then I climbed down and walked through the silent garden to my house. Many a time did I stop at places where I had once seen her pass or had lain in the shade thinking of her.

In and about my little house everything looked as it did when I had left it the day before. The garden stood bare and plundered, indoors the great ledger lay open, my violin, which I had almost forgotten, hung thick with dust on the wall. From the window opposite a ray of morning sunshine was at that very moment glancing like a lightning flash over the strings. The sight of it struck a chord in my heart. 'Come,' said I, 'come, my faithful fiddle! This is not the world for such as you and me!' I took the violin from the wall, left ledger, slippers, dressing gown and parasol where they were and wandered away, as poor as I had come, out of the house and down the gleaming highroad. I cast many a glance behind me; I had a curious feeling, sad and yet overjoyed as a bird escaping from its cage. When I had walked a fair stretch I put up my fiddle in the free open air and sang:

> God's ways alone are my ways,
> Larks, streams and fields and wood,
> 'Twixt earth and heaven all my days,
> I know His ways are good.

The castle, the garden and the towers of Vienna had vanished behind me in the morning haze, countless larks rejoiced high above me in the sky as I set off past the hills, past the bright towns and villages, away down towards Italy.

3

Soon, however, I was in trouble for I did not know the right way and had not given it a thought. In the still of that early hour there was not a person in sight whom I might have asked and not far from where I stood the highroad divided into several branches leading far, far away over the high hills as if to the end of the world, making me dizzy from looking.

At last a peasant came in sight along the road, going, I think, to the church, as it was Sunday, and wearing an old-fashioned topcoat with big silver buttons and carrying a long Spanish cane topped with a very heavy silver knob which flashed from afar in the sunlight. I at once asked him with much courtesy: 'Can you please tell me, which is the road which leads to Italy?' The peasant stopped, looked at me, then reflected with his underlip jutting forward and looked at me again. I said once more: 'To Italy—where the oranges grow.' 'Ah, what do I care for your oranges!' said the peasant and strode bravely on. I had imagined the man to have had better manners, for he had quite a grand look about him. What was I to do now? Turn back and return to my village? ,Then the people would have pointed their fingers at me and the boys would have jumped round me crying: 'Welcome back from the big wide world! What is it like out there? Have you brought us back some gingerbread from your travels?' The porter with the imperial nose, who knew a great deal of the world, had often said to me: 'Sir, Italy is a beautiful country where God provides all; there you may lie down on your back while the grapes grow into your very mouth and if you are bitten by the tarantula you will dance with most uncommon agility, however unskilled you may be at dancing.' 'No! To Italy, to Italy!' I cried joyously and ran off, without a care for the several roads, along the route which happened to lie at my feet.

When I had strolled on for a while I saw to the right of the road a most beautiful orchard, where the morning sunlight shone so gaily between the trunks and branches that it seemed as though the grass were laid with a golden carpet. Seeing no one about I climbed over the low fence and lay comfortably down in the grass beneath an apple tree, for all my limbs still ached from having spent last night up a tree. From there I could see far over the landscape whence, it being Sunday, the sound of bells came ringing from afar over the silent fields and everywhere countryfolk decked in their best were wending their way through bush and meadow to church. My heart was cheered, the birds sang above me in the tree and I thought of my mill, of my gracious lady and how far, far away it all now lay—until at last I fell asleep. I dreamed that my lady was walking through the countryside, or rather floating slowly towards me to the sound of the bells and trailing long white veils which floated in the morning sunshine. Then it seemed as if we were no longer far from home, but in the shadow of the mill in my village. There too all was so still and empty, as when the people are all gone to church on Sunday with only the organ music to be heard through the trees, that my heart ached. Yet my lady was so kind, held me by the hand, walked with me and amidst all this loneliness she sang the same beautiful song which she used always to sing to her guitar early in the morning at the open window. As she did so I saw her image reflected in the calm mill-pond, looking a thousand times more beautiful, but with eyes strangely large which stared at me so fixedly that I was almost afraid. All at once the mill-wheel began to splash and turn, at first in slow, single strokes then faster and louder until the mill-pond darkened and rippled, my lady turned quite pale, her veils grew longer and longer and waved in long, fearful trails like mist high into the sky; the roaring grew louder, joined with what seemed like notes from the porter's bassoon until suddenly I awoke with a violently beating heart.

A wind had indeed arisen and was blowing gently through the apple tree above me, but the noise of roaring and rumbling was neither the mill nor the porter but that same peasant who earlier had refused to show me the way to Italy. Now, though, he had doffed his Sunday suit and stood before me wearing a white smock. 'Aha,' said he, as I was still wiping the sleep from my eyes, 'perhaps he wants to steal some of those oranges here and that's why he's a-trampling my good grass instead of going to church, the sluggard!' I was angry, but only because this boor had woken me up. Furious, I leaped up and quickly retorted: 'Berate me, would you? You do not know it, but I have been a gardener—and a toll-keeper, and if you had driven into town you would have been obliged to doff your greasy night-cap to me; I had a house of my own and a red dressing gown with yellow spots.' But this rustic clod was not impressed and only stuck his arms akimbo and said: 'What might he want, then? Eh? Eh?' I now saw that he was a short, stocky, bow-legged fellow with goggling, protruding eyes and a red, slightly crooked nose. As he continued to say nothing more but 'Eh? Eh?' and each time took a step nearer to me, I was suddenly overcome by such a curious and uncanny feeling of anxiety that I quickly made off, jumped over the fence without looking round and galloped headlong over the fields at such a pace that my fiddle rang in my pocket.

When at last I stopped to draw breath the orchard and the valley were no more to be seen and I found myself in the midst of a beautiful wood. I did not, however, give it much thought as the whole scene now began to anger me, especially the way the rude fellow had called me 'he' and for a long while I cursed silently to myself. Deep in these thoughts I marched rapidly on, moving further and further from the highroad and into the hills. The woodland track along which I had taken flight came to an end and now there was only a narrow and scarcely trodden footpath before me. There was no one to be seen and not a sound to be heard, but the walking was pleasant, the tree-tops rustled and the birds sang most sweetly. I commended myself, therefore, to God's guidance, pulled out my violin and played through all my favourite pieces, the sound echoing gaily through the lonely wood.

My playing did not last for long, though, as I stumbled

every minute over some vexing tree root. In time I began to grow hungry and there seemed no end to the wood. Thus I wandered about the whole day long and the sun was already slanting through the tree-trunks when I finally reached a little grass-grown valley surrounded by hills and carpeted with red and yellow flowers, over which countless butterflies flickered in the gold of the evening. Here it was as lonely as if the world lay a hundred miles away. There was only the chirping of the crickets and a shepherd lying in the tall grass and blowing on his shawm with heart-breaking melancholy. He has a fine life, thought I, the idle fellow—while the likes of us must work ourselves to a shred and forever keep alert. As there ran between us a clear brook which I could not cross, I shouted to him from the far side to tell me where the nearest village lay. He made no move except to stick his head a little out of the grass; he pointed towards the next wood with his shawm and calmly went on playing.

I marched bravely on, as dusk was beginning to fall. The birds, which had all the time been singing mightily until the last rays of the sun glimmered through the wood, were suddenly silent and I almost began to feel afraid in the endless, lonely rustling of the forest. At last I heard the distant bark of a dog. I quickened my pace, the wood thinned out and soon I saw between the trees a square of green where a host of children were tumbling noisily round a big lime tree in its centre. On one side of the square was an inn, in front of which a few peasants were seated round a table, playing cards and smoking. On the other side, before a doorway, were some young lads and

31

several girls, their arms folded in their aprons, gossiping together in the cool evening air.

Without much ado I drew my fiddle from my pocket and quickly played a gay country dance as I walked out of the wood. The girls looked up in surprise and the old men laughed so loud that it echoed through the wood. But when I reached the lime tree and had leaned against it, still playing, a subdued muttering and whispering began to run right and left among the younger folk; the lads finally put away their Sunday pipes, each one took a partner and before I had noticed it the young peasants were swinging gaily all about me, the dogs barked, the skirts flew and the children were standing round me in a circle staring curiously at my face and my fingers as I fiddled away.

Only when the first tune was over was I able to observe the enlivening effect of a piece of good music: the peasant lads, who before had been sitting about on benches, pipe in mouth, stretching their stiff limbs before them, were now all at once as if transformed; they let their bright kerchiefs dangle low from their buttonholes and pranced so nimbly around the girls that it was a joy to see. One of them, who had a somewhat superior air, fished for a long time in his waistcoat pocket to make sure that the others would notice it and finally produced a small silver piece which he tried to press into my hand. I did not care for this, even though I was for the moment penniless. I told him to keep his money, that I played only for the joy of being in company again. Soon afterwards a comely young lass came up to me with a big tumbler full of wine. 'Musicians are always glad of a drink,' she said to me with a friendly laugh and her pearl-white teeth flashed so charmingly between her red lips that I could have kissed them there and then. She dipped her little beak into the wine, her eyes flashing at me over the glass as she did so and handed me the tumbler. I drank it to the dregs and began to play afresh, at which they all spun gaily round me once more.

The elders had meanwhile finished their game and even the young people began to grow tired and to drift away until gradually the village green before the inn grew empty and still. The girl too, who had handed me the wine, started back towards the village but she walked very slowly and glanced round now and again as if she had forgotten something. Finally she stopped and looked for something on the ground, but I noticed that whenever she bent down she looked back at me under her arm. Having learned a little of life during my stay at the castle, I sprang after her and said: 'Have you lost something, fairest mam'selle?' 'Oh no,' said she, blushing all over, 'it was only a rose—would he like it?' I thanked her and stuck the rose into my buttonhole. She gave me a very friendly look and said: 'He plays so beautifully.' 'Yes,' I said, 'it is something of a gift from God.' 'Musicians are very rare creatures hereabouts,' went on the girl, her eyes firmly downcast. 'He might earn himself a good stipend here—my father also plays the fiddle a little and loves to hear tell of foreign parts—and my father is very rich.' Then she laughed and said: 'If only he would not make such grimaces when he's fiddling!' 'Dearest maiden,' I replied, 'firstly: kindly cease to address me as "he". Then as for my head-wagging—that is something common to

33

all us virtuosi.' 'Oh, is it now,' answered the girl. She was about to say something more, but at that moment there came a terrible crash from the inn, the door opened with a loud creak and a thin fellow shot out like a ramrod fired from a gun and the door was immediately slammed after him.

At the first sound the girl ran away like a hind and vanished into the darkness. The figure outside the door nimbly picked himself up and began to hurl curses at the tavern at such a rate that I was amazed. 'What,' he shouted, 'I—drunk? I haven't paid my score chalked on that smoke-blackened old door? Rub it out, rub it out! Was it not I who shaved you only yesterday, holding your head over the cooking-ladle which you bit in half when I nicked your nose? The shave makes one mark—the cooking-ladle spoilt, another mark—the plaster for your nose, yet another mark—how many more strokes of the chalk do you expect me to pay, you dog? Very well then, the whole village, the whole world for aught I care can go unshaven. For my part you may all walk around with beards, so God cannot tell Jew from Christian at the day of judgement. Yes, you may all go and hang yourselves by your beards, you hairy country boors!' Here he broke into pitiful weeping and howled quite miserably: 'Must I drink water like a wretched fish? Is that neighbourly feeling? Am I not a man and a master surgeon-barber? Oh, I am in such a fury! And my heart full of such a love of my fellow men!' So saying he gradually drew away from the inn, as no sound came from within. When he saw me he ran towards me with outspread arms and I thought that this wild wretch was about to embrace me.

34

I jumped to one side, he stumbled on and I heard him long afterwards holding forth in language now coarse, now fine, into the darkness.

I, however, had much else to think of. The maiden who had given me the rose was young, pretty and rich; I could have made my fortune there in the wink of an eye. There would be mutton and pork, turkey and fat goose with apple stuffing—indeed, it was as if I saw the porter himself urging me on: 'Take it, toll-keeper, take it! Faint heart never won fair lady, nothing venture— nothing gain, a bird in the hand . . .'

With such philosophical thoughts I sat down on a stone on the village green, which was now quite deserted, for I did not dare to knock on the inn door for lack of money. The moon shone brilliantly, the rustling of the woods gently wafted over from the mountainsides and the sleep of the village in its valley under the moonlit trees was only occasionally broken as the bark of a dog was taken up by others. I gazed at the firmament, where sparse clouds sailed slowly through the moonlight and now and again a distant shooting star would fall. This same moon, I thought, was shining both on my father's mill and the count's stately white castle. There all has long been silent, my lady is asleep and only the fountains and the trees in the garden are still gently rustling as they ever did and no one there cares whether I am still alive or have met my death abroad. At this thought the world seemed all at once so terrifyingly vast and I so much alone that I could have wept from the bottom of my heart. After a while as I sat there I suddenly heard the sound of hoofbeats in the wood. I held my breath and listened as it came nearer and nearer until I could even hear the horses snorting. Soon two riders emerged from the wood, but halted at its edge and spoke earnestly and stealthily to one another, as I could see from the shadows suddenly cast on the moonlit village green. With long, dark arms they pointed now here, now there. How often when my mother used to tell me tales at home of wild forests and fierce robbers had I secretly wished to take part myself in such a story. Now my stupid, idle wishes were to be realized! Quietly I climbed as far as I could up the trunk of the lime tree where I was standing until I reached the first branch and quickly swung myself over. Just as I was dangling with half my body over the branch and was about to haul my legs up, one of the horsemen quickly trotted over the green behind me. I closed my eyes firmly among the greenery and stayed quite still.

'Who's there?' came the sudden cry from behind me. 'No one!' I shouted at the top of my voice, fearful that he had discovered me. Inwardly I could not help laughing at these fellows' disappointment when they turned out my empty pockets. 'Aha,' said the robber, 'then whose are those two legs hanging down?' There was nothing more to be done. 'Only a pair that belongs to a poor wandering musician who has lost his way,' said I and quickly dropped to the ground, for I was growing ashamed of hanging over the branch like a bent fork.

The rider's horse shied as I fell so suddenly from the tree. He patted its neck and said with a laugh: 'Well, we too have lost our way, so we are companions in misfortune. I thought that you might help us to find the way to B——. You shall come to no harm for it.' I protested in vain that I had no notion of where B—— might be, that I had best inquire at the inn or lead them down into the village, but he would not hear reason. He calmly drew from his belt a pistol, which glittered in the moonlight. 'My dear fellow,' he said in the most friendly fashion as he wiped the barrel of the pistol and then inspected it critically, 'you will, I am sure, be so kind as to go before us and lead the way to B——.'

I was in a pretty fix. If I found the way I would certainly fall among the robber band and be beaten because I had no money; if I did not find it I should also be beaten. I did not waste much time in thought, but took the first path I could see which led past the inn and out of the village. The horseman galloped back to his companion and both began to follow me at some distance, the blind leading the blind through the bright moonlit night. The path lay down the mountainside and through the forest. Now and again one could see over the tall, darkly waving pinetops far away into the deep, still valleys, occasionally a nightingale struck up, dogs barked in the distant villages. Down below a river could be heard splashing and occasionally flashed in the moonlight. The monotonous gait of the horses and the clinking and creaking of the riders' harness mingled with their ceaseless talk in a foreign language. The bright moonlight and the long shadows of the tree-trunks flickering on the two horse-men played such tricks that they seemed to be constantly changing shape—now bright, now black, now small, now as tall as giants. My thoughts were as confused as if I were in a dream from which there was no awakening. I kept up a firm pace, thinking that we must soon come out of the forest and the night.

At last long, reddish streaks began to flit across the sky, as lightly as when one breathes on a mirror, and a lark began to sing high above the silent valley. Suddenly this dawn greeting lightened my heart and all my fear was gone. The two horsemen stretched themselves, looked all around and seemed only now to realize that we might well be on the wrong road. They had a long talk together and it was clear that they were speaking about me, indeed, it even seemed as though one of them was beginning to grow afraid of me, perhaps thinking that I was a decoy posted to lead them astray in the wood. This amused me, for the lighter it grew the more my courage rose and we had just reached a beautiful open clearing in the woods, so I began to stare wildly round in all directions and gave a few whistles on two fingers as urchins do when they want to signal to each other. 'Stop!' shouted one of the horsemen, so suddenly that I jumped with fright. As I looked round I saw that they had both dismounted and tethered their horses to a tree. One walked rapidly up to me, stared at my face and burst into uncontrollable laughter. 'Why,' said he, 'I do declare its the gardener, or I should say the toll-keeper, from the castle.'

I gaped at him, but could not recall him, having been too busy to look at all the young gentlemen who used to ride in and out of the castle, but he continued, laughing all the while: 'This is splendid! You are foot-loose, as I see, we happen to need a servant—stay with us and you will have a post for life.' I was nonplussed and finally said that I had just undertaken a journey to Italy. 'To Italy?'

rejoined the stranger, 'but we too are going there!' 'Well, if that is so ...!' I cried and joyously pulled my fiddle from my pocket and struck up with such vigour that the birds in the wood all woke up. The stranger ran to his companion and rolled about in the grass with him as though gone mad. Then they suddenly stood still. 'By God,' cried one, 'I can see the church tower of B——! Why, we shall soon be down there!' He pulled out his watch, made it strike, shook his head and let it strike again. 'No,' he said, 'we cannot go yet, we would be too early and that could mean trouble.'

Thereupon they fetched cakes, roast meat and bottles of wine from their saddlebags, spread a brightly coloured cloth on the green grass, set to with gusto and shared it generously with me, which I greatly enjoyed since I had not eaten a proper meal for several days. 'But do you not,' said one of them to me, 'know who we are?' I shook my head. 'Well, let us introduce ourselves: I am Leonhard, a painter, and my friend here is called Guido—he is also a painter.'

In the dawn light I was now able to scrutinize the two artists more closely. One of them, Master Leonhard, was tall, slim, brown-haired, with jolly, flashing eyes. The other was much younger, shorter and finer-built, dressed in the old German fashion, as the porter used to call it, white collar and bared neck hung around with his dark brown locks, which he was constantly shaking away from his handsome face. When he had eaten his fill of breakfast he picked up my fiddle, which I had laid on the grass beside me, sat down on the branch of a felled tree and plucked at the strings with his fingers. Then he sang to this accompaniment, as clearly as a woodland bird, a song whose sound echoed through my heart:

> Dawn's first rays fly to the hill,
> Probe the valleys, misty, still;
> Now as rustling woods are waking
> Those who can their flight are taking.
>
> Now, the joyful man is out,
> Flings his hat up, starts to shout:
> If the source of joy is singing
> Let my voice with song be ringing!

As he did so the reddish glow of the dawn light played gracefully over his somewhat pale face and his black, passionate eyes. But I was so tired that the words and melody as he sang seemed to grow more and more confused until at last I fell asleep. When I gradually came to myself again, as if in a dream I heard the two artists still talking beside me and the birds singing above me while the rays of the dawning sun shone through my closed eyes, so that I saw a dull half-light as when the sun shines through red silk curtains. *'Come è bello!'* I heard one of them exclaim beside me. I opened my eyes and saw the young artist bending so closely over me in the sparkling morning light that I could see almost nothing but his big, dark eyes between his long, hanging locks. I jumped up to find that it was already broad daylight. Master Leonhard seemed to be somewhat peevish, with two angry lines marking his forehead, and he began to make haste to depart. The other artist only shook his curls from his face and calmly trilled a song as he untethered his horse until Leonhard too suddenly laughed aloud, seized a bottle which lay on the grass and poured the remains of its contents into our glasses. 'Here's to our safe arrival!' he cried; they clinked glasses with a merry sound and Leonhard threw the bottle high into the air, where it flashed gaily.

At last they were mounted and I too set off briskly. Before us lay a valley which stretched away out of sight, into which we began to descend. How it flashed and rustled, how joyously it all glittered! My head felt so light and cool that I could have flown down from the mountain into that magnificent vista before us.

4

And so adieu, mill and castle and porter! Now we were off, with the wind whistling past my hat. To right and left villages, towns and vineyards flew past so quickly that they seemed to flicker before my eyes; behind me in the coach were the two artists, before me four horses with a splendid postilion and myself, often bouncing inches into the air, high up on the box. It had happened thus: when we reached B——, at the very edge of the village a tall, gaunt, morose gentleman dressed in a green petersham coat came to meet us and with many a bow to the two artists led us into the village. There, beneath a tall lime tree in front of the posting-house, stood a magnificent four-in-hand ready harnessed. On the way Master Leonhard had mentioned that I should change my clothes, at which he drew some other clothes from his portmanteau and I was made to don a handsome new frock-coat and waistcoat which suited me nobly, except that they felt over-long and broad and flapped around me. I also acquired a new hat which shone in the sunshine as though it had been pomaded with fresh butter. Then the gloomy stranger led away the horses; the two painters jumped into the coach, I on to the box and we started just as the postmaster in his nightcap looked out of the window.

The postilion gave a merry blast on his post-horn and we were off and away to Italy.

Up there I enjoyed all the pleasures of a bird in the air without the labour of flying. I had nothing to do but sit on the box night and day and to fetch meat and drink to the coach from inns on the way, for the artists never stepped indoors and by day they closed the coach windows tight, as though the sunlight might injure them. Only occasionally did Master Guido stretch his head out of the window and chat to me in friendly fashion, when he would laugh at Master Leonhard, who could not bear this and always grew angry at our long talks. A few times I was nearly in trouble with my master, once when on a clear starry night I began to play my fiddle on the box, and then later because I could not help falling asleep. It was astonishing—I wished after all to see as much of Italy as possible—and would open my eyes every quarter of an hour, but no sooner had I looked around me for a while than the sight of those sixteen horses' hooves flickering and criss-crossing before my eyes brought me to such a mesmerized state that my eyes closed again and eventually I sank into such a fearful, irresistible sleep that there was no keeping awake. It might be day or night, rain or sunshine, Tyrol or Italy, I could do nothing for it but lean now left, now right, now backwards over the box, indeed I often dashed my head on the floor with such vehemence that my hat fell off and Master Guido shouted aloud from within the coach.

So without quite knowing how I had travelled half the way through that part of Italy known as Lombardy when we stopped one fine evening before a country inn. The

43

post horses from the neighbouring station would not be ready for a few hours, the artists alighted and were led to a private room to rest a little and write some letters. I was delighted at the respite and betook myself at once to the tap-room in order to be able to eat and drink again in peace and comfort. The place had a slovenly look about it. The maids walked around with matted hair and open kerchiefs draped round the yellowish skin of their necks. The inn servants, wearing loose blue overshirts, were seated at a round table eating their supper and now and again gave me a sideways glance. They all had short, thick plaited queues and looked as elegant as young gentlefolk. Here you are, I thought to myself as I assiduously went on eating, here you are at last in that country whence all those curious people used to come and sell mousetraps, barometers and pictures to the vicar. What can a man not learn when he once ventures forth from hearth and home!

As I sat eating and meditating, a little man, who until then had been sitting in a dark corner of the room over his glass of wine, suddenly scuttled over to me from his cranny like a spider. He was short and hunchbacked, with a grisly face with a long Roman nose and sparse red side-whiskers and his powdered hair stood up all round his head as though a storm had blown through it. He wore an old-fashioned, threadbare frock-coat, short velvet breeches and silk stockings turned quite yellow. He had been to Germany once and imagined that he understood German to perfection. He sat down beside me and pestered me with questions on this and that, while he constantly took snuff: Was I the *servitore*? When would we *arrivare*?

Did we go to *Roma*? I knew nothing of these matters myself and could not understand his double-Dutch. At last in distress I said to him '*Parlez-vous français?*' He shook his big head, which was a relief to me as I knew no French either. But these tactics could not throw him off: he had well and truly fixed his eye on me and pressed his questions without cease. The more we parleyed the less we understood of each other, then we finally grew quite heated and I began to feel that this signor was about to stab me with his sharp nose, until at last the maids who had overheard our babel-like discourse laughed us both heartily to scorn. I put down my knife and fork and went outside. In this alien land it was as if I with my German tongue had been sunk a thousand fathoms into the sea and all kinds of strange worms were squirming and rustling, staring and snapping at me.

Out of doors it was just the sort of warm summer night to go for a stroll. From the distant vineyards a vine-dresser could now and again be heard singing, lightning flashed occasionally from afar and the whole countryside trembled and rustled in the moonlight. At times I thought I noticed a tall, dark figure lurking behind the hazel bushes in front of the inn and peering through the branches, then all was still again. Suddenly Master Guido stepped out on to the balcony. He did not notice me, but struck up with great skill on a zither, which he must have found in the inn, and sang to it with the voice of a nightingale:

Man's loud joy at last is still,
Earth stirs gently as though dreaming,
Leaves are sighing, moonlight gleaming,
And the heart with secret skill

45

For old sadness now beats quicker,
Showers pass, dead moments flicker
Like the lightning on the hill.

I cannot tell whether he sang any more, because I had
stretched myself out on a bench in front of the tavern and
fell asleep in the warm night from sheer weariness.
Several hours must have passed before the post-horn
wakened me, after sounding long in my dreams before I
came to my senses. At last I jumped up, day was already
dawning over the mountains and the dew was soaking
my limbs. Only then did I recall that it was time for us to
leave. Aha, thought I, today it is my turn to do the waking
and the laughing at them. How Master Guido would
leap up with his sleepy head of curls when he heard me
outside. So I walked into the small garden close under
their window, turned once more towards the dawn's
glow and sang with a merry heart:

When the larks begin to rise,
Day approaches in the skies.
As the sun begins to peep—
Oh, how good it is to sleep!

The window was open, but all was quiet upstairs
except for the night wind blowing through the vines
which grew up to the window. 'What can this mean?'
I cried out in astonishment, ran indoors and through the
silent corridors to their room. There I had a shock. When
I opened the door all was empty: not a jacket, not a hat,
not a boot. Only the zither, which Master Guido had
played yesterday, still hung on the wall. On the table in
the middle of the room lay a full purse of money with a

note attached to it. I held it close to the light and could hardly trust my eyes, for in very truth it read in large letters: 'For the toll-keeper'!

What use, though, was it all to me if I were to lose my dear, kind masters? I shoved the purse into the capacious tail pocket of my coat, where it dropped as if into a deep well and nearly pulled me over backwards. Then I ran out, making a great deal of noise and waking all the maids and servitors in the house. They had no notion of what I wanted and thought I had gone mad, but soon they were as amazed as I had been when they saw that the birds had flown from their nest. Nobody knew anything of my two gentlemen. Only one maid—as far as I could gather from her signs and gesticulations—had noticed that Master Guido, while singing on the balcony the evening before, had suddenly cried aloud and rushed back into the room to his companion. On waking later that night she had heard the sound of horses' hooves, had looked out of the little window of her chamber and seen the hunch-backed signor, who had conversed with me for so long yesterday, galloping across the moonlit fields on a grey at such a speed that he flew in the air from his saddle, at which the girl had crossed herself, so much did he resemble a ghost riding on a three-legged horse. What was I to do?

Meanwhile our coach had long been waiting ready harnessed at the door and the postilion was impatiently blowing his horn fit to burst, for he had his timetable to consider which laid down the precise time at which he was due to arrive at the next posting-station. I ran once more round the whole house and called the two artists,

47

but there came no answer; the people from the inn all ran out in a crowd and gaped at me, the postilion cursed, the horses snorted, until at last I sprang, in utter confusion, into the coach. The ostler slammed the door behind me, the postilion cracked his whip and away I went once more into the wide world.

5

We drove on over hill and dale, night and day without cease. I had no time to gather my thoughts, for wherever we stopped fresh horses were waiting ready harnessed, I could not speak to the people and my sign language was useless; often when I was seated over an excellent meal at an inn the postilion would sound his horn, I would have to drop knife and fork and leap aboard the coach again without the least idea whither I was going nor why we should be travelling at such an exhausting pace.

Otherwise life was none too bad. I lay as if on a couch first in one corner of the coach and then in the other and saw a great deal of Italy and the Italians. Whenever we drove through a town I would lean out of the window on both arms and thank the people who politely doffed their hats to me, or I would wave to the girls at their windows like an old friend, whereupon they stared even harder and gaped after me long and curiously.

At last I received a great fright. I had never counted the money in my purse, I had been everywhere obliged to pay out a great deal to the postmasters and innkeepers and before I knew it the purse was empty. At first I decided to jump out of the coach and run away as soon as we passed through a deserted wood, but then I regretted the

49

thought of leaving the splendid coach in which I could gladly have travelled on to the very end of the world.

Thus I sat, deep in thought and incapable of finding a solution to my dilemma, when the coach suddenly took a side turning from the highroad. I shouted out of the window to the postilion to ask where he was going, but to whatever I said the fellow only answered: '*Sì, sì, signore!*' and drove on heedless of sticks and stones in a manner which threw me from side to side of the coach.

I could not understand the reason for our change of route, as the highroad at that point ran through a splendid landscape towards the setting sun, like a glittering sea in its richness and glory, whereas in the direction which we had now taken lay only harsh mountains broken by dismal gorges where darkness was already setting in. The further we drove the wilder and more desolate the region grew. At last the moon appeared from behind some clouds and shone all at once so brightly on the trees and cliffs that it was grim to behold. We could only drive slowly along the narrow, stony gorges and the endless, monotonous rattling of the coach resounded from the rocky sides far into the silent night as though we were driving into a great tomb. The only sounds were the constant roaring of unseen waterfalls deep in the forest and the incessant hooting of screech-owls: 'Come *too*, come *too*!' After a while it seemed to me as if the coachman, who, as I now noticed for the first time, was no longer a uniformed postilion, began to give many an uneasy glance around him and drove faster; once as I leaned right out of the coach a horseman came suddenly out of the undergrowth, jumped clean across the path in front of our horses and was immediately lost again in the woods on the other side. I was amazed, for as far as I could perceive in the bright moonlight it was the same hunch-backed manikin on his grey who had stabbed at me with his aquiline nose in the tavern. The coachman shook his head and laughed aloud at this wild exhibition, but then turned round to me and spoke long and volubly, of which I unfortunately understood nothing, and then drove on faster than ever.

I was very relieved when soon afterwards I saw a light flickering in the distance. Gradually more and more lights appeared, they grew larger and brighter and finally we drove past a few smoke-blackened huts clinging like swallows' nests to the cliff-side. As the night was warm the doors stood open and I could see the brightly lit rooms within, in which ragged vagabonds squatted round the fire like dark shadows. On we rattled through the still night and up a stony path which began to climb a steep hillside. At one moment tall trees and dangling bushes covered the sunken path, at another we could again see the heavens and down below the vast, silent ring of mountains, forests and valleys. On the peak of the mountain there stood in the brilliant moonlight a great and ancient castle, set with innumerable turrets. 'God help me!' I cried, inwardly heartened and full of expectation to discover at last where I was to be brought. It was another half-hour at least before we finally reached the castle gates. We entered through a broad, round tower whose upper works were almost in ruins. The coachman gave three cracks of his whip, which echoed through the old castle and sent a sudden swarm of jackdaws fluttering in terror from every crack and cranny and whirling through the air with loud cries. Thereupon the coach rolled in through the long, dark gateway: the horses' hooves sent sparks flashing from the cobbles, a great dog barked, the coach thundered between the vaulted walls, the jackdaws still screaming—and so with much sound and fury we made our entrance into the narrow, paved castle courtyard.

A curious posting-station! I thought to myself as the coach drew to a stop. The coach doors were opened from outside and a tall old man with a small lantern stared grimly at me from beneath thick eyebrows. He took me by the arm and helped me, as though I were a great lord, to alight from the coach. Before the great door stood an extremely ugly old woman in black smock and jacket, with a white apron and a black cap from which a long tassel hung down to her nose. She held a large bunch of keys dangling at her hip and in the other hand an old-fashioned sconce with two lighted wax candles. As soon as she saw me she made a deep curtsey, babbling questions the while. I could understand none of it, but bowed awkwardly to her, feeling ill at ease.

Meanwhile the old man had been shining his lantern all round the coach, muttering and shaking his head because there was no sign of trunk or baggage. Then the coach-man, without demanding a tip from me, drove the coach away into an old shed which stood open on one side of the courtyard. The old woman, however, bade me with signs to follow her. With her candles to light the way she led me through a long, narrow passage and up a small stone staircase. As we passed the kitchen a few young maids put their heads inquisitively round the half-open door and stared at me, beckoning and nodding mysteriously to each other as though they had never seen a male creature in their lives. At last the old woman opened an upstairs door, at which I was at first quite nonplussed, for it led into a large and beautiful, indeed magnificent, room adorned with gold on the ceiling, with splendid flowered tapestries on the walls depicting all sorts of figures and large flowers. In the middle stood a table laid with roast meats, cakes, salad, fruit, wine and sweets which cheered me to the heart. Between the two windows hung a huge mirror reaching from floor to ceiling.

I must say that I found it all most pleasing. I stretched myself a few times and walked up and down the room in properly noble manner, but I could not long resist looking at myself in such a grand mirror. In truth Master Leonhard's new clothes suited me handsomely and since my stay in Italy I had acquired something of a fiery glance, but otherwise I was still the same beardless milksop that I had been at home, with only a few strands of fluff beginning to show on my upper lip. / ↑↓?

All this time the old woman continued to mouth away with her toothless gums, for all the world as if she were chewing the tip of her pendulous nose. She bade me be seated, stroked my chin with her withered fingers, and called me *poverino*! at which she gave me a roguish look from her reddened eyes, and pulled the corners of her mouth half way up her cheeks, and finally left the room with a deep curtsey.

As I sat down at the table a young and pretty maid entered to serve me. I tried out many a gallant discourse with her, but she could not understand me and only stared with curiosity at my delight over the meal, which was most delicate. When I had eaten my fill and stood up again, the maid took a light from the table and led me into another room. There was a sofa, a little mirror and a magnificent bed hung with green silk curtains. I signed to her, asking whether I might lay down in it? She nodded 'Yes', but I could not do so as she remained beside me as if nailed to the spot. Finally I fetched myself a large glass of wine from the room in which I had dined and wished her '*Felicissima notte!*' for I had by then learned that much Italian, but as I drained the glass in one draught she suddenly burst into a fit of suppressed giggling, blushed all over, walked into the dining-room and out at the door. What is there to laugh at? I thought in amazement; I do believe all Italians are mad.

I was still afraid lest the postilion should start blowing his horn again. I listened at the window, but all was quiet outside. Let him blow, I thought as I undressed and lay down in the splendid bed. It was as if I were swimming in milk and honey. The old lime tree rustled outside in the courtyard and now and again a jackdaw would suddenly fly up from the roof until at last, in deep satisfaction, I fell asleep.

6

When I awoke again the first rays of the morning were already playing over the green curtains above me. I could not properly remember where I was. It seemed to me that I was still driving in the coach and that I had dreamed of an old castle in the moonlight, of an old witch and her pale daughter. At last I jumped out of bed, dressed myself and while doing so looked all round the room. Then I noticed a little tapestried door which I had not seen yesterday. It was only ajar, I opened it and espied a neat little room that looked most inviting in the light of the dawn. Some women's clothes were thrown untidily over a chair and beside it lay the girl who had served me at table the evening before. She was still fast asleep and she had lain her head on her bare white arm, over which fell her black curls. If she knew that the door was open! I said to myself and returned to my bedroom, shutting and bolting the door behind me lest the girl should be ashamed and take fright when she awoke. Outside there was not a sound to be heard. Only an early woodland bird was sitting outside my window, singing his morning song on a tuft that grew out of the wall. 'No,' said I, 'you shall not shame me by being the first to rise and sing your praises to God.' I picked up my fiddle, which I had laid on the table yesterday, and went out. All was still deathly quiet in the castle and it was long before I found my way out through the dark passages.

When I stepped out in front of the castle I entered a large garden, which descended half the mountainside in broad terraces. As a garden, however, it was a poor piece of work. The paths were all overgrown with tall grass, the boxwood topiary figures were untrimmed and stretched out such long ghostly noses or yard-long pointed caps that one might have taken fright to see them in the twilight. There was even washing hung over some broken statues atop a dried-up fountain, here and there someone had been burning charcoal in the midst of the garden and a few dull flowers were growing in untidy confusion beside tall, ragged weeds, the haunt of bright lizards. A lonely vista of mountain after mountain peak was the only sight to be seen through the tall and ancient trees.

After strolling around for a while through this wilderness, I noticed on the terrace below me a tall, thin, pale youth in a long brown cowled habit walking up and down with arms folded. He appeared not to have seen me. Shortly afterwards he sat down on a stone bench, drew a book from his pocket and began reading in a very loud voice as though he were preaching, now and again gazing heavenwards and resting his head in melancholy fashion on his right hand. I stared at him for a long time until I grew curious to know why he made such odd grimaces and walked up to him. He had just heaved a deep sigh and leaped up in fright as I approached. He was embarrassed, as indeed was I, neither of us knowing what we should say and exchanging endless bows until he finally fled into the bushes with long strides. The sun had meanwhile risen over the forest, I jumped up on to the bench and for pure pleasure struck up on my fiddle until it echoed far down the silent valleys. The old woman with the bunch of keys, who had anxiously been searching for me all over the castle to summon me to breakfast, now made her appearance on the terrace above me and was amazed that I played so well on the fiddle. The grim old man of the castle joined her and was quite astonished; finally came the maids, who all stood above me in wonderment while I fingered the strings and swung my fiddlestick with ever greater skill and speed, playing cadenzas and variations until I finally wore myself out.

Strangely enough no one at the castle spoke of my journeying further; it was indeed no posting-inn, but belonged, as I learned from the maid, to a rich count. On the many occasions that I asked the old woman for the count's name and where he lived, she would merely smirk as she had on the first evening that I came to the castle and wink at me as furiously as if she were out of her senses. When once, on a hot day, I drank a whole bottle of wine, the maids giggled when they brought me another bottle and even when I demanded a pipe of tobacco, describing it to them by signs, they all burst out into loud and unreasonable laughter. But most mysterious of all was a serenade which was to be heard frequently and always on the darkest nights beneath my window, consisting of no more than occasional soft chords on a guitar. Once, however, I thought that I heard someone call out 'Psst! Psst!' while the music was playing. I leaped out of bed and stuck my head out of the window 'Hullo! Who is that out there?' I called down, but no one answered and I heard nothing but the sound of something running quickly away through the bushes. My shout caused the big dog in the courtyard to bark a few times, then all was still again and after that the serenade was never heard again.

Otherwise my life here left nothing to be desired. Ah, the good old porter! He knew what he was talking about when he used to say that the raisins in Italy grew into one's very mouth. I lived in that lonely castle like an enchanted prince. Wherever I went the people showed me great deference, although by now they all knew that I had not a farthing in my pocket. I only had to say: 'Table, spread yourself!' and there stood a delicious meal ready for me—rice, wine, melons and Parmesan cheese. I delighted in the food, slept in the magnificent four-poster, went for walks in the garden, made music and even helped with the gardening. Often I would lie for hours in the tall grass of the garden and the thin youth (he was a student, a relative of the old woman, who was here for his vacation) in his long cassock walked round me in a wide circle, murmuring aloud from his book like a magician—which always sent me to sleep. So the days went by, until at last so much good food and drink began to make me melancholy. The lack of occupation made my limbs quite slack and I felt as if I should fall apart from idleness. It was thus that I was sitting one sultry afternoon in the top of a tall tree, which stood on a slope, gently rocking myself on the branches over the deep, still valley. The bees buzzed around me through the leaves, otherwise all was motionless, not a soul was to be seen on the mountainsides while far below me the cattle were at rest in the tall grass of the woodland meadows. Then from far away came the sound of a post-horn over the wooded hilltops, at first hardly to be heard and then louder and clearer. All at once an old song came to my mind, which I had learned at home at my father's mill from a wandering apprentice, and I sang:

A wanderer's heart will not grieve him
Who fares with his love, his own:
For others rejoice and would leave him,
A stranger bereft, alone.

Dark tree, whisper tales of the old times,
Of fled moments, fine and dear.
Ah my homeland! which in these cold times
Is far away from me here.

I love now in starlight to wander—
Stars shone when I sought her before—
I hear in that nightingale, yonder,
The song near my darling's door.

The morning's great joy always thrills me:
First, its stillness on the plain,
Then for mountains a yearning fills me,
Where I greet my dear home again.

It seemed as though the post-horn in the distance was trying to accompany my song. As I sang it came nearer and nearer through the mountains, until at last its sound could be heard coming from the castle courtyard itself. I jumped quickly down from the tree. The old woman was already coming towards me, carrying an open parcel. 'Something has come for you,' she said and handed me a neat little letter from the parcel. It bore no address, but I quickly opened it. All at once I went as red in the face as a peony and my heart beat so furiously that the old woman noticed it, for the letter was from—my gracious lady, whose handwriting I had seen many times on notes addressed to the estate bailiff. Her message was quite short: 'All is now well, all obstacles are overcome. I made secret use of this opportunity to be the first to send you these glad news. Come, hasten back. It is so desolate here and I cannot live since you have left us. Aurelia.'

As I read this my eyes swam with delight, with fear and unspeakable joy. The sight of the old woman, who was smirking at me again in her repellent fashion, made me suddenly shy and I fled like an arrow to the loneliest corner of the garden. There I threw myself down into the grass under some hazel-bushes and read the letter once more, repeating the words aloud until I had them by heart and then read them again and again as the sunbeams danced through the leaves over the letters, making them into golden, red and pale green blossoms before my eyes. Did she eventually not marry, I thought, was the unknown officer perhaps her brother, or is he now dead, or am I mad? 'What matter?' I cried at last and sprang up. 'One thing is clear—she loves me, yes, she loves me!'

When I crept out of the bushes the sun was beginning to set. The sky was red, the birds were singing merrily in the woods and the valleys were shimmering in the evening glow, but my heart was a thousand times brighter and happier!

I called to the castle that they should bring my supper out into the garden this evening. They should all, the old woman, the gloomy old man and the maids, come outside and share my table under the trees. I took up my fiddle and played in between eating and drinking, which made them all gay: the old man's grim frown vanished as he downed glass after glass of wine, the old woman mumbled incessantly God knows what rubbish and the maids began to dance with each other on the grass. Finally even the pale student appeared out of curiosity, threw a few scornful glances at the spectacle and made as if to depart again with great dignity. I jumped smartly to my feet, caught him unawares by his long cassock and waltzed him vigorously around. He tried hard to dance in the modern manner and made such efforts to keep time that the sweat poured down from his face and the long skirts of his cassock flew round us like a wheel. But he gave me such curious looks from his squinting eyes that I grew quite afraid of him and suddenly let him go again.

The old woman would have liked to discover the contents of the letter and why I was so suddenly cheerful today, but it was all too complicated to explain to her. I merely pointed to a pair of cranes which were at that moment flying through the air above us and said that I must away again, away and away into the far distance! At that she opened wide her dried up old eyes and stared like a basilisk, first at me and then at the old man. Then I saw them both putting their heads together whenever I turned away, talking most earnestly and occasionally squinting sideways at me.

I could not but notice this and tried urgently to think what they might be hatching between them. I grew quiet; as the sun had long since set I wished them all a good night and went pensively up to my bedroom.

I felt so happy and so disturbed that I paced up and down in my room for some time. Outside the wind was rolling heavy black clouds over the castle turrets and even the nearest mountaintops were scarce to be seen in the darkness. Then I thought that I could hear voices down below in the garden. I put out my light and stationed myself by the window. The voices seemed to come nearer, but they were talking very softly. All at once a small lantern, carried by a cloaked figure, sent out a long ray. I was now able to make out the grim castle bailiff and the old housekeeper. The light shone over the old woman's face, which I had never seen looking so ghastly, and on a long knife which she was holding in her hand. I could also see that they were both looking up at my window. Then the bailiff drew his cloak tightly round him and all was once more dark and still.

What, I wondered, are they doing out in the garden at this hour? I shuddered as I recalled all the tales of murder that I had ever heard in my life, tales of witches and robbers who cut men down in order to eat their hearts. As I sat there in thought, the sound of footsteps came first up the stairs, then softly, softly along the long corridor towards my door, accompanied now and again by the sound of whispering voices. I quickly sprang behind a large table at the other end of the room, with the aim, as soon as anything should move, of picking it up and running with all my force for the door. But in the darkness I knocked over a chair, which made a fearful clatter; at once all was quiet outside. I listened from behind the table, staring all the while at the door as though I might pierce it with my sight until my eyes were starting from my head. After I had remained there for a while, so still that one could have heard the flies walking on the wall, I heard someone softly putting the key into the keyhole from outside. I was about to rush forward with my table when whoever it was turned the key three times round in the lock, carefully pulled it out and softly withdrew along the corridor and down the stairs.

I took a deep breath. Oho, thought I, so they have locked you in to catch you more easily when you have fallen asleep. I quickly examined the door. I was right; it was securely locked, as was the other door, beyond which slept the pretty, pale maid. This had never happened since I had been at the castle. I was a prisoner in a foreign land? My dear lady would now be sitting at her window and looking out over the silent garden towards the turnpike, wondering whether I would come strolling along past the toll-booth with my fiddle, the clouds were flying across the sky, time was passing—and I could not escape from here! My heart ached so that I could no longer think what to do. All the time I felt, whenever the leaves rustled outside or a rat scurried under the floorboards, that the old woman had secretly entered through a concealed door in the tapestry and was lurking and creeping about in the room with her long knife. As I sat anxiously on the bed I suddenly heard, for the first time for a long while, the serenade beneath my window. At the first notes of the guitar it was just as though a ray of sunlight shone through my soul. I flung open the window and called softly down that I was awake. 'Psst! Psst!' came the answer from below. I wasted no more time in thought but seized the letter and my fiddle, swung myself out of the

63

window and climbed down the crumbling old wall by holding on to the tufts that grew out of the cracks. However, a few rotten bricks gave way, I started to slip and slide down, faster and faster, until I finally landed with such a thump on both feet that my brainbox rattled.

Scarcely had I reached the garden in this way than I felt myself embraced with such vehemence that I cried aloud. My good friend quickly put his finger to my mouth, seized me by the hand and led me out of the shrubbery into the open. There with amazement I recognized the tall student, who was carrying the guitar slung round his neck on a broad silk band. In great haste I conveyed to him that I wanted to find my way out of the garden. He seemed to know this already and led me by all manner of concealed by-ways to the furthest turret at the bottom of the garden wall. This too was locked, but the student had made provision for this; he drew out a large key and carefully unlocked the door.

As we stepped out into the forest and I was about to ask him the best way to the nearest town, he suddenly cast himself down on one knee before me, raised his hand high and started to curse and swear in a manner terrible to hear. I had no notion of what he wanted and could only hear how he repeated *iddio* and *cuore* and *amore* and *furore*. When he began, though, to crawl nearer and nearer towards me on both knees, I had a sudden feeling of horror and saw in truth that he must be insane; I ran, without looking round, away into the thickest part of the wood.

I could hear the student running after me, raging and

64

shouting. Soon another and rougher voice could be heard in answer from the castle. I thought that they were now certain to set off in my pursuit. I did not know the way, the night was dark and I might easily fall into their hands again. I therefore climbed to the top of a tall fir tree to await a better opportunity.

From where I was I could hear voice after voice awakening at the castle. Torches appeared up above and threw their wild glare over the old masonry of the castle walls and far out over the mountains into the dark night. I commended my soul to God, for the wild uproar grew ever louder and nearer. At length the student, bearing a torch, ran past the trunk of my tree, the skirts of his long cassock flying in the wind; then they all seemed gradually to turn towards another flank of the mountain, the voices grew fainter and fainter and only the wind was again heard rustling through the silent forest. Then I climbed down from the tree and ran, breathless, into the night and towards the valley.

7

For a day and a night I hurried on, for I imagined that I could hear them shouting down the mountain and chasing me with torches and long knives. On my way I learned that I was only a few miles distant from Rome. This news gave me a shock of joy, for even as a child at home I had heard so many wonderful tales of glorious Rome, and when I lay in the grass before the mill on Sunday afternoons and all around was still, I imagined Rome to be like the great clouds sailing above me, with wonderful hills and chasms, with golden gates and tall shining towers on which angels in golden raiment stood and sang. Night had long since fallen again and the moon was shining brilliantly when at last I stepped out of the wood on to a hill and suddenly saw the city in the distance before me. Far away was the glint of the sea, the infinite sky flashed and sparkled with countless stars and beneath it lay the Holy City, which could be seen as no more than a long swathe of mist like a sleeping lion on the silent earth, the mountains round about like dark giants standing guard.

As I walked on I came first to a great lonely tract of heath, where all was as grey and as still as the grave. Only here and there stood a pile of decaying masonry or a dry, wonderfully twisted bush; many a night bird flapped across the sky and always my own shadow strode, long and dark, in the loneliness beside me. They say that an ancient city, in which is the tomb of the lady Venus, lies buried here and that at times the old heathen will rise from their graves to walk the heath at dead of night to lead travellers astray. But I kept going straight ahead, in fear of naught, for the city rose before me ever clearer and more splendid and the tall castles, the gates and golden domes shone so gloriously in the bright moonlight, as though in truth angels in golden raiment were standing on the roofs and singing out into the silent night.

At last I began to pass the first little houses, then went through a magnificent gateway into the famous city of Rome. The moon shone between the palaces as though it were bright daylight, but the streets were all empty, only here and there in the soft night air lay a ragged figure as though dead, asleep on some flight of marble steps. The fountains splashed in quiet squares and gardens along the street rustled softly, filling the air with vivid scent.

As I strolled along, so full of pleasure, of moonlight and well-being that I knew not where to turn, suddenly from deep within a garden came the sound of a guitar. By God, thought I, that must be the mad student with the long habit who has been secretly following me! Then a lady in the garden began to sing with surpassing beauty. I stood as if bewitched, for it was the voice of my beautiful, my gracious lady and the same Italian song which she had so often sung at her open window.

All at once the happy past came back to my thoughts

with such force that I could have wept bitter tears; there again was the silent castle garden in the early morning and myself so happily ensconced behind the shrub—before that stupid fly had decided to crawl up my nose. I could restrain myself no longer. I climbed up the gilded wrought-ironwork, over the gate and swung myself down into the garden from whence came the song. Then I noticed that a slim white figure was standing in the distance behind a poplar; at first she stared at me in amazement as I climbed over the lattice-work, but then ran off so quickly through the dark garden towards the house that I could hardly make out her feet as she fled in the moonlight. 'That was her!' I cried, and my heart beat with joy, for I had recognized her at once by her swift little feet. It was unfortunate that in jumping down from the gate I had slightly twisted my right foot and shambled a few paces on one leg before I could run after her towards the house. In the meantime, though, door and window had been bolted fast. I knocked timidly, listened and knocked again. I seemed to hear a sound of whispering and giggling from indoors and once I even thought that I saw two bright eyes sparkling in the moonlight between the shutters. Then all was still again.

Of course, she does not know who I am, thought I and took out my fiddle which I always carried with me, walked up and down with it on the pathway in front of the house, played and sang the song of the gracious lady and played all the songs which I used to play on fine summer nights in the castle garden or on the bench in front of the toll-house, loud enough to be heard from the castle window. But all to no avail; no one stirred in the whole house, so at last I sadly put away my fiddle and lay down on the threshold of the house, for I was very tired from my long march. The night was warm, the flowerbeds in front of the house gave off a delicious scent and deeper within the garden a fountain splashed without cease. I thought of sky-blue flowers, of lovely dark green, lonely valleys, where spring water babbled and streams flowed and gaily coloured birds sang wonderfully—until at last I fell fast asleep.

When I awoke the morning air was chilling me in every limb. The birds were already awake and were twittering on the trees around me as though to laugh me to scorn. I jumped up and looked all around me. The fountain in the garden was still splashing, but not a sound was yet to be heard indoors. I squinted through the green shutters into one of the rooms. There was a sofa and a large round table covered with a grey linen cloth, chairs stood in neat rows round the walls; outside, however, the shutters were let down over all the windows as though the whole house had been uninhabited for years. A shudder of fear overcame me at this lonely house and garden and at the thought of the white figure of the night before. I ran, without looking round, through the silent bowers and pathways and quickly climbed up the lattice gate. But I stopped and sat as if bewitched when all at once I caught sight of the gorgeous city from the top of the gate. The morning sun was flashing and sparkling over the roofs and into the long, silent streets; the sight made me cry out in delight and, full of joy, I jumped down into the street. But whither should I turn in this great, unknown city? The confused events of the night and the

Italian song of my gracious lady were still running through my head. At last I sat down on the stone fountain in the middle of a deserted square, washed my eyes clean in the clear water and sang as I did so:

> Were I a bird on high,
> I know what I should be singing;
> And with two wings to fly
> I know where I'd be winging.

'Aha, my merry fellow, you sing like a lark at sunrise!' I suddenly heard a young man, who had walked up to the fountain as I sang, say to me. Hearing these words spoken so unexpectedly in German it was just as though it was a Sunday morning and the bells of my own village had suddenly started to ring. 'God be with you, fellow-countryman,' I cried and, full of cheer, jumped down from the stone fountain. The young man smiled and looked me up and down. 'But what in the world are you doing here in Rome?' he finally asked. I did not quite know what to say, for I did not care to tell him that I had just been leaping over gates after my dear lady. 'I am travelling around,' I replied, 'in order to see something of the world.' 'I see,' said the young man and laughed aloud, 'then we are in the same trade, you and I, for I too am seeing the world and painting it as I go along.' 'So you are an artist!' I shouted joyfully, remembering Master Leonhard and Master Guido. But the young man interrupted me before I could say more. 'I think,' said he, 'that you should come and have breakfast with me, for it would give me great pleasure to do your likeness.' I readily accepted and set off with the artist through the empty streets, where only occasional shutters were yet open and where now a pair of white arms, now a sleepy little face appeared in the fresh morning air.

For a long while he led me round and about through a maze of narrow, dark alleyways, until we finally slipped into an old, smoke-blackened house. There we climbed up one dark stairway and then another, as though we were climbing to heaven itself. We now stood before an attic doorway and the artist began to search furiously in all his pockets, but early that morning he had forgotten to lock his door and had left the key inside the room, for as he told me on the way he had been out before daybreak in order to see that district of the city before sunrise. He only shook his head and kicked the door open. It was a large and very long room in which one could have held a dance, had not everything lain all over the floor. Boots, paper, clothes and knocked-over pots of paint lay in utter disorder; in the middle of the room were some large step-ladders, of the sort one uses to pick pears, and a number of large pictures were leaned against the walls. On a long wooden table was a dish, containing bread and butter and a blob of paint; beside it stood a bottle of wine.

'First you must eat and drink, fellow-countryman!' said the painter. I was about to spread myself a few slices of bread and butter, but there was no knife. We had first to rummage for a long while among the papers on the table before we finally found it under a large parcel. Thereupon the artist flung open the window to let a pleasant gush of fresh morning air into the room. There was a glorious view right across the city and away over to the mountains, where the morning sun was casting its joyful rays over white farmhouses and vineyards. 'Here's to our cool green land of Germany up there over the mountains!' cried my artist friend, taking a swig from the wine bottle and handing it to me. I politely followed suit and silently greeted my beautiful homeland a thousand times over. Meanwhile the painter had pulled a wooden easel, on which was stretched a large sheet of paper, closer to the window. On the paper was a drawing, in bold black strokes, of an old hut. In it sat the Holy Virgin with a beautiful face, at once joyous and sad. At her feet in a little nest of straw lay the child Jesus, looking happy but with great, serious eyes. Outside on the threshold of the open hut knelt two shepherd boys with staff and wallet. 'Do you see,' said the painter, 'I shall put your head on one of the shepherd boys, so people will see your face and, God willing, it will still give them pleasure when you and I are both long in our graves and are kneeling as quietly and joyfully before the Holy Mother and her son as these happy young lads in the picture.' Then he seized an old chair which, as he picked it up, broke in pieces, leaving him holding nothing but half the chair-back. He quickly fitted it together again, then pushed it in front of the easel, made me sit on it and turn my face slightly sideways. For a few minutes I sat quite still without moving, but—I do not know why—I could not hold the pose for long; now I felt an itching here, now there. The broken half of a mirror hung opposite me and I could not keep myself from staring into it while he painted and, out of boredom, making every kind of grimace. The painter, who had noticed it, finally burst out laughing and gestured to me to stand up again. He had finished drawing my face on the shepherd boy and it looked so handsome that even I found my own likeness most pleasing. He continued to draw away industriously in the fresh, cool morning air, singing a little song as he worked and now and again glancing out at the open window to the glorious view. I meanwhile cut myself another slice of bread and butter and walked up and down the room with it, inspecting the pictures that were propped up against the wall. Two of them pleased me particularly. 'Did you also paint these?' I asked the painter. 'Would that I had!' he replied. 'They are by the famous masters Leonardo da Vinci and Guido Reni—but what do you know about them!' I was angered by his last words. 'Oh,' said I, 'I know both of these masters as well as I know my own pockets.' At that his eyes opened wide. 'How so?' he quickly asked. 'Well,' said I, 'I have been travelling with them day and night, on foot, on horseback and by coach, so fast that the wind whistled past my hat; I lost them both in an inn and then drove on alone in their coach at double speed, the coach bouncing over the most fearful stones on two wheels and ...' 'Aha! Aha!' the painter interrupted me and stared at me as if I were mad. Then he suddenly burst out into loud laughter. 'Ah,' he cried, 'now I understand. You made the journey with two artists called Guido and Leonhard?' When I answered in the affirmative, he hastily jumped up and stared at me again very closely from top to toe. 'I do believe,' he said, at last—'do you play the violin?' I slapped my tail-pocket, making the fiddle ring. 'In truth,' said the painter, 'a countess from Germany has been here, inquiring in every corner of Rome after two artists and a young musician with a fiddle.' 'A young countess from Germany?' I cried out in excitement. 'Is the porter with her?' 'That I cannot tell,' replied my artist. 'I only saw her a few times at the house of a friend, who lives outside the city. Do you know her?' he went on, suddenly lifting the canvas cover from a large picture standing in the corner. I felt at that moment as one does when the shutters are opened on a dark room and the morning sun floods in to dazzle one's eyes; it was—my beauty, my gracious lady! She stood in a garden in a black velvet dress, lifting her veil from her face with one hand and gazing calmly and happily over a glorious distant prospect. The longer I looked the more strongly I felt as though it were the castle garden, the trees and branches were swaying gently in the wind and in the distance I could see my little toll-house, the turnpike stretching far into the green countryside, the Danube and the distant blue mountains. 'It is she, it is she!' I cried out at last, seized my hat, ran down the many stairs and out at the door, only just hearing the astonished artist shouting after me that I should come back towards evening, when we might perhaps learn more!

8

I ran through the city with reckless speed, in order to show myself again at that house in the garden where my lady had sung last night. In the meantime the streets had come to life, gentlemen and ladies were out walking in the sunshine, bowing and greeting one another on all sides, gorgeous carriages rattled along between them and from every church tower the bells were ringing for mass, the sound echoing marvellously in the clear air above the throng. I felt as if I were drunk with joy and the noise of the crowd and in my gladness I ran straight ahead until eventually I no longer knew where I was. It was like magic, as if the silent square with the fountain, the garden and the house had been merely a dream and everything had vanished from the earth at the break of day. I could not ask anyone, because I did not know the name of the square. At last it began to grow very sultry, the sun's rays struck the cobbles like singeing arrows and people began to retire indoors; everywhere shutters were closed and all at once the streets were dead. At last, in despair, I cast myself down in front of a large, handsome house, before which a colonnaded balcony threw its broad shadows, and gazed first at the silent city, which had taken on a positively sinister look in the sudden solitude of bright midday, then again at the deep blue, almost cloudless sky, until at last I too fell asleep from utter weariness. I dreamed that I was lying in an empty green meadow in my own village, a warm summer shower was falling and glistening in the sun, which had just set behind the mountains and as the raindrops fell on the grass they turned into a mass of brilliant flowers which covered me in their profusion.

How astonished I was, however, when I awoke and saw a host of beautiful fresh flowers really lying beside me! I sprang up, but could discover nothing unusual except that high up in the house above me was a window full of scented herbs and flowers and behind them a parrot, chattering and screeching without cease. I collected the scattered flowers, tied them together and put the bouquet into my buttonhole. Then I struck up a conversation with the parrot, for I was pleased to watch him climbing up and down in his gilded cage with all sorts of grimaces, tripping clumsily over his big toe at every step. Before I knew it he cursed me for a '*furfante*'. Although he was no more than a heathen beast, I was nevertheless vexed. I cursed him in return; finally we both grew heated and the more I swore at him in German, the more he gurgled away at me in Italian.

Suddenly I heard someone laugh behind me. I quickly turned round. It was the painter of this morning. 'What madcap tricks are you playing now?' he said. 'I have been waiting for you for half an hour. The air is cooler now, we must go to my friend's garden outside the city where you will find many of your fellow-countrymen and perhaps learn some more about the German countess.'

I was delighted at this and we set off at once on our walk, while for long I could hear the parrot still cursing away at my back.

After a long climb outside the city up narrow, stony footpaths between farmhouses and vineyards, we came to a small garden on a plot of high ground where several young men and girls were seated at a round table in the open. As soon as we entered they all signed to us to be quiet and pointed over to the other side of the garden. There in a great, green-grown bower sat two beautiful ladies facing one another at a table. One was singing, the other accompanying her on the guitar. Between them behind the table stood a cheerful man, now and again beating time with a little wand. The evening sun sparkled through the vine leaves, now over the wine bottles and fruit with which the table in the bower was covered, now over the full, round, dazzling white shoulders of the lady with the guitar. The other lady was as if enraptured, as she sang in Italian with such abandon that the tendons on her neck stood out.

Just as she was sustaining a long cadenza with her eyes turned heavenwards and the man beside her with baton raised was awaiting the exact moment when she would take up the beat again, and not a soul in the garden was daring to breath, suddenly the garden gate flew open wide and a flushed girl, followed by a young man with delicate, pale features burst in, engaged in a violent quarrel. The frightened conductor stood still like a petrified magician with wand raised, although the singer had long since broken off her extended trill and had angrily stood up. All the others hissed furiously at the

77

newcomers. 'Barbarian,' one of those at the round table shouted at him, 'you are running right into the middle of the brilliant tableau, enacted just as the blessed Hoffman on page 347 of the *Ladies Companion for 1816* so beautifully described the finest picture by Hummel shown at the 1814 exhibition of art in Berlin!' But this had no effect. 'Oh, fie,' returned the young man, 'on your tableaux of tableaux! I paint my own paintings for others to look at and keep my own girl for myself! And so it will be! Oh false, oh faithless one!' said he, turning again to the wretched girl. 'You criticize—yet in painting you can judge only its worth in silver and in poetry only its weight in gold! You want no dearest one—only what is dear! Henceforth instead of an honest painter I wish you an old duke with a whole mine full of diamonds on his nose, the glint of silver on his bald pate and a golden parting in his few remaining hairs! Come, out with that cursed note which you tried to hide from me before! What devilment are you up to now? Who is it from and to whom is it addressed?'

The girl, however, stood up to him bravely and the more zealously the others surrounded the angry young man and loudly attempted to console and calm him, the madder and more heated he grew from the noisy crowd, especially since the girl herself was not inclined to hold her tongue, until at last she fled from the milling throng and suddenly threw herself quite unexpectedly at my breast to seek my protection. I at once adopted the appropriate stance, but as the others in the crowd were paying no attention to us, she suddenly turned her little head up towards me and quickly whispered quite calmly and softly into my ear: 'Oh you, you dreadful toll-keeper! It is for your sake that I have to suffer all this. There, take the fatal note and hide it—it tells you where we are living. Be there at the appointed hour. When you pass the city gate, the deserted street on your right hand!' Such was my amazement that I could not utter a word, for now when I could see her properly I recognized her at once: she was in very truth the pert little chambermaid from the castle who had brought me the bottle of wine on that beautiful Sunday evening. I had never seen her looking so pretty as now when she leaned against me, quite flushed, with her dark curls hanging over my arm. 'But my dear mam'selle,' I said in astonishment, 'how do you come to be . . .' 'For heaven's sake be quiet, be quiet now!' she replied and sprang away from me to the other side of the garden before I could grasp what had happened.

Meanwhile the others had by now almost forgotten the original quarrel, but were cheerfully continuing to argue among themselves as they tried to prove to the young man that he was drunk, which was not seemly for an artist with pretentions to honour. The stout, lively man from the bower, who was—as I later learned—a great connoisseur and lover of the arts and whose pleasure it was to participate as a keen amateur, had thrown away his wand and was strolling around in the thick of the crowd, his fat face positively glistening with amiability, in an attempt to mediate and smooth it all over, whilst he continued to regret the spoilt cadenza and the beautiful tableau which he had been at such pains to arrange.

79

My heart, though, was as light as it had been on that blessed Saturday when I had played on my fiddle long into the night with the wine-bottle at my open window. There seemed to be no end to the noise and confusion; I took out my violin and without pausing long to think I struck up an Italian dance which they dance up in the mountains and which I had learned at the lonely old castle in the forest.

At once every head was raised. 'Bravo, bravissimo, a delicious inspiration!' cried the gay connoisseur and at once ran from one to another in order to arrange a rustic 'divertissement', as he called it. He himself led the dance, offering his hand to the lady who had played in the bower. He began to dance in a highly artificial style, describing all manner of figures on the grass with the points of his toes, shaking regular trills with his feet and from time to time making quite passable leaps in the air. He soon had enough, though, for he was somewhat corpulent. His leaps grew ever shorter and clumsier, until he finally retired from the circle, coughing mightily and never ceasing to wipe away the sweat with his snow-white handkerchief. Meanwhile the young man, who had now quite recovered his humour, had fetched some castanets from the inn and before I knew it, they were all dancing pell-mell under the trees. The sun, although set, still cast a few red rays of afterglow between the dark shadows and over the old masonry and the ivy-grown, half-collapsed columns at the end of the garden, whilst in the other direction, far below the vineyard terraces, could be seen the city of Rome basking in the evening glow. There they all danced under the branches in the clear, still air and my heart danced with them to see the slim girls, the chambermaid in their midst, weave between the foliage, arms arching upward like heathen wood-nymphs as they gaily clashed their castanets in time to every step. I could no longer restrain myself, but leaped into their midst and cut a few merry capers as I fiddled away.

I had no doubt been leaping around in the circle for some time without being aware that the others had begun to grow tired and were gradually drifting away from the grassy dance-floor. Then I felt a violent tug at my coat-tails. It was the chambermaid. 'Stop playing the fool,' she said softly, 'you are jumping about like a billy-goat! Take my advice, read your note and follow me soon; the fair young countess is waiting.' And with that she slipped through the garden gate in the twilight and quickly vanished among the vineyards.

My heart was beating so hard that I would have liked to spring after her. Fortunately, as it had now grown dark, the waiter lit a large lantern by the garden gate. I stepped up to the light and pulled out the note. Scribbled on it in pencil was a description of the gate and the street, as the chambermaid had told me. It read: 'Eleven o'clock by the little door.' How many long hours stretched ahead till then! I was nevertheless about to set out on my way at once, for I could rest no longer, but at that moment the painter, who had brought me here, approached me. 'Have you spoken to the girl?' he inquired. 'I can no longer see her anywhere; she is the chambermaid of the German countess.' 'Hush, hush,' I replied, 'the countess is still in Rome!' 'Well, so much the better,' said the artist, 'come and drink her health with us!' And with that he dragged me back into the garden, in spite of all my resistance. It had in the meantime become empty and deserted. The convivial guests, each with his sweetheart on his arm, were strolling back to the city and they could be heard among the vineyards, chattering and laughing in the still of the evening, the voices fading further and further into the distance until at last they were lost in the valley among the rustling of the trees and the stream. I was left behind, alone except for my artist friend and Master Eckbrecht—for such was the name of the other young painter who had earlier caused such a rumpus. The moon shone down brilliantly on to the garden between the tall, dark trees, a lamp on the table before us flickered in the wind and glinted on the many pools of wine spilled on the table. I was made to sit down and my artist companion chatted with me, asking me whence I had come, about my journey and my plans for the future. Master Eckbrecht had seated the pretty young girl from the inn on his lap after she had placed some bottles on our table. He laid the guitar in her arm and began teaching her to strum a song on it. Her little hands soon learned the knack and together they sang an Italian song, he and the girl singing a verse in turn, which sounded splendid in that beautiful still evening. When the girl was called away, Master Eckbrecht leaned back on the bench with the guitar, put up his feet on a chair before him and, heedless of us, sang to himself a score of beautiful German and Italian songs. The stars came out in their glory in the clear firmament, the whole neighbourhood was bathed in silver moonlight and I, quite forgetting the painter beside me, began thinking of my gracious lady

82

and of my distant homeland. Now and again Master Eckbrecht was obliged to re-tune the guitar, which always vexed him greatly. He twisted and tugged at the instrument until suddenly a string snapped, at which he threw away the guitar and jumped up. Only now did I perceive that my painter had meanwhile laid his arm on the table and fallen fast asleep. Master Eckbrecht flung round his shoulders a white cloak, which hung on a branch near the table; a sudden thought struck him and he gave a few sharp glances at my painter and then at me, sat firmly down on the table opposite me, cleared his throat, straightened his neckerchief and began to deliver me a speech.

'Beloved listener and fellow countryman!' he said. 'As the bottles are now almost empty and morality is incontestably the citizen's first concern when virtue is in decline, I feel myself driven, out of sympathy to a fellow countryman, to bring to your attention certain moral precepts. One might think,' he went on, 'that you were a mere youth, whereas your frock-coat is long past its prime; one might perhaps suppose that you were leaping about like a satyr this evening. Some might even maintain that you were a vagabond, because you are strolling about the countryside and playing the fiddle; but I pay no heed to such superficial judgements: I judge by your pointed nose and I say you are a wandering genius.' I was angered by his teasing manner and I was about to retort, but he left me no time to speak. 'There,' he said, 'you see how you have already puffed yourself up on that little bit of praise. Examine yourself and ponder on the dangerous profession you have chosen! We geniuses—for I am one too—care as little for the world as the world cares for us, rather we stride on heedlessly into eternity in our seven-league boots, with which we are born. Oh, it is a deplorable, uncomfortable posture, one leg in the future with nothing but dawn light and the faces of unborn children around you and the other leg in the midst of the *Piazza del Popolo* in Rome, where everybody loves you when things are going well and clings so tightly to your boot that you feel your leg is being pulled off! And so much agony, so much wine-drinking and going hungry—all for the sake of immortality and eternity! Look at my fellow artist there on the bench, who is also a genius; he finds life such hard work that he will be worn out before he reaches eternity. Yes, my dear fellow genius, you and I and the sun, we were all up early this morning, we brooded and painted all day long and everything was fine—and now the sleepy night is sweeping her sable arm across the world and has smothered all our colours.' He went on and on in this vein, looking as pale as a corpse in the moonlight, his hair in disorder from so much dancing and drinking.

His wild rhetoric filled me with horror and when he turned and addressed the sleeping artist I seized the opportunity and slipped unnoticed round the table, out of the garden and sped thankfully away past the vineyards and down through the broad moonlit valley.

From the city the clocks could be heard striking ten. Behind me I could still hear a few guitar chords ringing through the silent night and occasionally the voices of the two artists, who had also set off homewards, could be heard in the distance. I therefore ran as fast as I could,

84

lest they overtake me and ply me with more questions.

At the city gate I immediately turned to the right into the street I was seeking and hurried on, with beating heart, between the silent houses and gardens. I was amazed, however, when all at once I came upon the square with the fountain, which in daylight that morning I had been unable to find. There in the glorious moonlight stood the lonely house in its garden and my gracious lady, too, was in the garden singing again the same Italian song that she had sung yesterday evening. In great excitement I ran first to the little door, then to the front door and finally to the garden gate, but everything was locked. Only now did I recall that it had not yet struck eleven. Vexed though I was at the slow march of time, for the sake of polite behaviour I did not wish to climb over the garden gate as I had done the evening before. I thus walked up and down for a while in the deserted square and finally sat down again, pensive and full of silent expectation, on the edge of the stone fountain. The stars were twinkling in the sky, all was still and deserted in the square as I listened entranced to the singing of my gracious lady in the garden, her song mingling with the babbling of the fountain. Suddenly I caught sight of a white figure, coming from the other side of the square and making straight for the little doorway into the garden. I stared hard at it through the flickering moonlight—it was the wild artist in his white cloak. He pulled out a key, unlocked the door and in a flash he was in the garden.

This artist had piqued me from the very beginning with his extravagant talk; now I was quite beside myself with anger. This pathetic genius is obviously drunk again,

85

thought I, he has acquired the key from the chambermaid and now he intends to creep up on my lady, betray her, attack her—and so I rushed through the little doorway, which he had left open, and into the garden.

As I entered all was silent and deserted within. The door of the summer-house was open, a milky-white beam of light shone out and played on the grass and the flowers in front of the doorway. From where I stood I stared inside. There, in a magnificent green chamber only barely lit by a white lamp, lay my gracious lady, her guitar on her arm, on a silken chaise-longue, all innocent of the dangers lurking outside.

I had not looked for long before I noticed the white figure stalking cautiously behind the bushes towards the summer-house. All this time my lady was singing with such sadness that it melted the very marrow of my bones. I hesitated no longer, broke off a stout branch and charged with it straight for the white cloak, shouting aloud '*Mordio!*' in a voice that made the whole garden tremble.

The artist, seeing my unexpected approach, took to his heels with a fearful scream. I screamed even louder, he ran towards the house, myself in pursuit—I had almost got him when I caught my foot in some stupid flower-stems and fell flat on my face in front of the door.

'So it is you, you fool!' I heard a voice shout above me. 'You almost frightened me to death.' I picked myself up and as I wiped the sand and earth out of my eyes, the chambermaid was standing before me, the white cloak having fallen from her shoulders with her last bounds. 'But,' said I in amazement, 'was not the artist here?'

86

'Indeed he was,' she replied in her pert voice, 'at least his cloak was, which he lent to me when I met him at the gate because I was cold.' Aroused by the noise, my lady too had jumped up from her sofa and came toward us. My heart thumped as if it would burst—but what was my horror when I looked closely and all at once saw instead of my beautiful, gracious lady a total stranger!

She was a somewhat tall, corpulent, powerfully-built woman with a proud, aquiline nose and arching black eyebrows, handsome though intimidating. She looked at me so majestically with her great flashing eyes that I was stricken helpless with awe. In utter confusion I could do nothing but bow and try to kiss her hand, but she snatched her hand away and said to the chambermaid something in Italian which I could not understand.

In the meantime the noise of our encounter had begun to waken the whole neighbourhood. Dogs barked, children started to cry, whilst here and there men's voices could be heard coming nearer and nearer the garden. Then the lady gave me another look as if she would bore through me with her two burning orbs, turned quickly back into her room with a haughty, false laugh and slammed the door in my face. The chambermaid pulled me away from the door and began dragging me towards the garden gate. 'Well, you have made a fool of yourself again,' she said angrily to me as we went. By now I was feeling aggrieved. 'Devil take you,' said I, 'was it not you yourself who told me to come here?' 'But of course,' cried the chambermaid, 'my countess does her best to be kind to you, throws flowers over you from the window, sings songs for you—and *this* is her reward! You are impossible; when good fortune comes your way you greet it with nothing better than kicks.' 'But,' I replied, 'I was expecting the countess from Germany, my gracious lady.' 'Oh,' she interrupted me, 'she has long since returned to Germany, still cherishing your stupid love for her—so if I were you I should run after her. She is pining for you; she and you may play the fiddle together and gaze at the moon—do anything, but never let *me* see you again!'

Now a terrible noise and disturbance arose behind us. Men with clubs were climbing over the wall from the next-door garden, others were cursing and searching the pathways, desperate night-capped faces stared here and there in the moonlight and looked over the hedges as if the devil and his horde were hiding somewhere in the bushes. The chambermaid acted quickly. 'There, there is the thief!' she cried to the men, pointing towards the opposite side of the garden. Then she quickly pushed me out of the garden and slammed the gate behind me.

Once more I stood, alone as God made me under the heavens in that empty square, just as I was when I had arrived only the day before. The fountain, which had seemed to splash gaily in the moonlight as though angels were climbing up and down it, still played on but now I had lost all delight in it. I resolved to turn my back for ever on faithless Italy with its mad artists, its oranges and its chambermaids and within the hour I was marching through the gate and out of the city.

9

The faithful guardian hills are stern:
· 'Whose steps disturb this quiet dawn—
Whose steps from foreign lands are drawn?'
But I their stony glare return,
And laugh for joy with swelling breast,
And cry aloud to break their rest,
Password and war-cry sounding far:
'Long live Austria!'

The mountain guards perceive their son.
Now streams sing welcome, woods and vales,
And birdsong greets me from deep dales
Where Danube's flashing waters run.
And glad to see me at this hour
I think I spy far Stephen's tow'r.
But if I'm wrong: it's now not far—
'Long live Austria!'

Standing on a high mountain from whence one catches
the first sight of Austria, I was joyfully waving my hat
and singing the last verse of my song when all at once
from the woods behind me came the sound of sweet
music from a wind band. I turned round and saw three
young men in long blue cloaks, one of them playing an
oboe, the second a clarinet and the third, wearing an old
three-cornered hat, playing a French horn. They began
to accompany my singing with such gusto that the whole
wood echoed. Not to be outdone I pulled out my fiddle

and played and sang with them. At this, one looked dubiously at the other, and the horn-player was the first to deflate his puffed-out cheeks and put down his horn; finally all three ceased playing and stared at me. Surprised, I too stopped and gazed at them in return. 'We thought, sir,' said the horn-player at last, 'that because you wore such a long frock-coat you were an Englishman on his travels who had come here on foot to admire the beauties of nature; we hoped to earn ourselves a few pence for the road. But it seems that you are yourself a musician.' 'A toll-keeper, if truth be told,' I replied. 'I come straight from Rome, but since I have collected no tolls for a long time I have managed to pay my way with my violin.' 'It earns little enough these days,' said the horn-player, who had meanwhile returned to the wood and was using his tricorne to fan a little fire that they had lit. 'Wind instruments are better,' he went on. 'When some gentleman sits down to eat at noon and we step unexpectedly into the gabled porch and all three of us begin to blow with all our might—a servant at once comes dashing out with money or food, simply to be rid of the noise. But would you not care to take some refreshment with us?'

With the fire crackling cheerfully in the wood, we sat down in the fresh morning air in a circle on the grass; two of the musicians removed from the fire a small pot containing coffee and milk mixed together, brought out bread from their coat-pockets and took it in turns to sip from the pot and dip in their crusts. It was a pleasure to see how they relished it. The horn-player, however, said: 'I cannot abide these black slops.' So saying he handed me the half of a large double slice of bread and butter and then produced a bottle of wine. 'Would you care for a mouthful, sir?' I took a generous draught, but put the bottle down straightaway with the most fearsome grimace, for it tasted like vinegar. 'The local vintage,' said the horn-player, 'but you, sir, will have ruined your German palate in Italy.' At that he rummaged in his knapsack and finally drew out from among all kinds of rubbish a tattered old map emblazoned with the emperor in full regalia, his sceptre in his right, the orb in his left hand. He carefully spread it out on the ground, the others drew closer and they discussed which route they should take. 'The vacations will soon be over,' said one, 'we must turn to the left at Linz if we are to reach Prague in good time.' 'But tell me,' cried the horn-player, 'who will you find there to listen to our music? Nothing but forests and coal-miners, no taste for art and not a hope of a decent free bed.' 'Oh, fiddlesticks!' countered the other, 'it is just the peasants that I prefer; they know where the shoe pinches and they are not so particular when you blow a wrong note now and again.' 'That shows that you have no *point d'honneur*,' said the horn-player, '*odi profanum vulgus et arceo*, as the Latins have it.' 'Well, at least we must choose a route where there are a few churches,' put in the third, 'then we may put up for the night at the vicarage.' 'I humbly beg your pardon,' said the horn-player, 'but they give precious little money and precious long sermons exhorting us to cease this idle vagabondage and to apply ourselves instead to the sciences, especially when they think they see in me a future colleague. No, no, *clericus clericum non decimat*. But why should we be in such haste? Our professors are still sitting in Karlsbad and do not keep term too carefully themselves.' 'Yes, *distinguendum est inter et inter*,' answered the second musician, '*quod licet Jovi, non licet bovi!*'

I saw now that they were students from Prague and felt a proper respect for them, particularly for the way the Latin tripped off their tongues. 'And you, sir, have you studied?' the horn-player asked me. I answered modestly that I had always wished to take up my studies but had lacked the funds. 'That makes no difference,' cried the horn-player, 'we too have neither money nor rich friends, but heaven helps him who helps himself. *Aurora musis amica*, which means in plain German that you should not spend too much of your precious time over breakfast. But when the bells ring out at noon from steeple to steeple and from hill to hill over the city and the students burst shouting out of their gloomy old college and swarm down the streets in the sunlight—then we run over to the good Brother Cook at the Capuchin friary and find the table laid for us. Even if it is not laid, there is a bowl of stew for each one, we take it gratefully, we eat and we polish up our Latin at the same time. So you see, sir, we study, as it were, from hand to mouth. And when at last it is vacation time again and the others drive or ride away home to their parents, we set off with our instruments under our cloaks, through the streets and out at the city gate—and the world is ours.'

As he described his life a great sadness came over me that such learned people as they should be all alone in the world. I thought of myself, of how I was in much the same plight myself and the tears started to my eyes. The horn-player stared at me. 'I like my life,' he went on again, 'I would not care for travelling as the rich do—horses and coffee, clean beds, night-caps and bootboys all bespoken in advance. That is the beauty of it, that when we set off at daybreak with the birds of passage flying high above us we never know whose chimney shall smoke for us that day nor what fortune may have in store for us by that evening.' 'Yes,' said the other, 'and when we arrive and bring out our instruments we spread joy around us and when we stop at noon at some country mansion and blow a serenade in the porch, the maids dance and the master leaves the dining-room door ajar, the better to hear the music, and through the crack comes the clatter of plates and the smell of roast meat served among the cheerful bustle and the young ladies at table almost twist their necks off from craning to see the musicians outside.' 'Forsooth,' cried the horn-player, his eyes flashing, 'let those who wish sit indoors and con their books—we meanwhile are studying God's own picture-album. Believe me, sir, it is we who will make parsons of the right mettle, we who can match the peasants in telling a tale and bang the pulpit so hard that the turnip-heads down in their pews will burst with shame and exaltation!'

As we talked I felt a great wish to be a student myself. I could not have enough of their talk, for I love to converse with learned men, as there is often profit in it. On this occasion, however, the conversation never grew interesting, for one of the students was in some distress that the vacation would so soon be over. He promptly put together his clarinet, laid some music across his knees and began practising a difficult passage from a mass, which he was due to play in the church band on his return to Prague. There he now sat, fingering and puffing away and often blowing such painfully wrong notes that I could not hear myself speak.

Suddenly the horn-player pointed at the map beside him and exclaimed in his bass voice: 'I have it!' The clarinettist looked up for a moment from his industrious blowing and stared at him in astonishment. 'Listen,' said the horn-player, 'not far from Vienna there is a castle; at that castle is a porter and that porter is my cousin! We must go there, brothers of the road, pay our respects to my dear cousin and he will see to it that we are put on the right road for the next stage of our journey.' When I heard this I jumped up. 'Does he not play the bassoon,' I cried, 'and is he not tall and upright in bearing with a great nobleman's nose?' The horn-player nodded and I embraced him with such joy that the tricorne fell from his head and we resolved there and then to take the posting-wherry and sail down the Danube to the castle of my fairest countess.

As we reached the riverbank all was ready for sailing. The fat innkeeper, before whose inn the sailing-barge had moored for the night, was standing stout and cheerful in his front doorway, which he filled completely, sending out a volley of jokes and shouts of farewell, while a girl's head stuck out at every window to say goodbye to the sailors who were loading the last packages aboard. An elderly gentleman in grey overcoat and black scarf, who also intended to take ship, was standing on the bank and talking very earnestly to a slim young lad in front of him mounted on a magnificent English thoroughbred and

94

wearing long leather hose and a short scarlet jacket. To my surprise I noticed that now and again they both looked in my direction and seemed to be talking about me. Finally the old man laughed, the slim youth flicked his riding-crop and galloped off through the fresh morning air, racing against the larks above him to be off and away over the shining hills.

The students and I had meanwhile combined our resources of cash. The captain laughed and shook his head when the horn-player paid our fares entirely in coppers, which we had laboriously collected together from our pockets. I shouted with joy to see the Danube before me again; we jumped aboard, the captain gave the signal and away we sailed down-river between the sparkling hills and meadows. The birds sang in the woods and from both sides came the sound of morning bells from distant villages, whilst an occasional lark added his joyous song from high in the air. The chorus was completed by the chirping and twittering of a canary on board our ship.

The canary belonged to a pretty girl who was sailing with us. She had put down the cage beside her and under her other arm she held a bundle of clothes. There she sat, in prim silence, glancing first at her new travelling shoes which peeped out from beneath her skirt, then down at the water, while the morning sunlight shone on her white forehead and her neatly parted hair. I noticed that the students would gladly have struck up a conversation with her, for they were constantly walking past her. The horn-player cleared his throat and straightened his neckerchief or his three-cornered hat as he went by, but they lacked the right sort of courage and every time they approached her the girl cast down her eyes.

She appeared to be particularly embarrassed by the elderly gentleman in the grey overcoat, who had seated himself on the other side of the ship and whom she obviously took for a cleric. He was holding a breviary from which he was reading, but often looked up at the beautiful landscape. The gold tooling and the many brightly-coloured pictures of saints in his book shone gorgeously in the morning sunshine. He observed everything that was happening on board and had soon recognized the birds by their plumage, for it was not long before he addressed one of the students in Latin, whereat they all three approached him, doffed their hats and replied likewise in Latin.

I had meanwhile taken up station in the very bow of the ship, where I amused myself by letting my legs dangle over the water and watched as the ship clove its way forward through the foaming, rushing water. Now a tower, now a castle would loom up among the green of the banks, would seem to grow and grow until at last it vanished astern. If only I had wings! I thought and from sheer impatience I drew out my beloved violin and played all my favourite pieces which I had learned at home and in my days at the castle of my gracious lady.

Suddenly I felt a hand on my shoulder. It was the clerical gentleman, who had put away his book and had been listening to me for a while. 'How now,' he said to me with a laugh, 'our master of the revels must not forget to eat and drink.' He then bade me put away my fiddle, invited me to take a bite with him and led me to a

96

delightful little bower which the sailors had constructed in the middle of the ship from birch and pine branches. There he had ordered a table to be set up and I, the students and the young girl took our places on barrels and bales around it.

The reverend gentleman unpacked a large joint of roast meat and some slices of bread and butter, which were neatly wrapped in paper, and produced several bottles of wine from a box together with a beaker of silver, which was gilded inside; he poured out, tasted it first, sniffed it, sipped it again and then passed it round to each of us in turn. The students sat bolt upright on their barrels and ate and drank very little, so much were they in awe of their host. The girl, too, scarcely dipped her little mouth into the beaker, gazing shyly at me and at the students as she did so, but the oftener she looked at us the bolder she gradually became.

She finally told the clergyman that she was leaving home for the first time to enter service and that she was travelling to the castle of her new master and mistress. I blushed as she said this, for she named the castle of my gracious lady. So this was to be my future chambermaid! thought I and stared at her, feeling slightly faint. 'There is soon to be a great wedding at the castle,' said the clerical gentleman. 'Yes,' replied the girl, who would have liked to hear more of the story, 'they say that it is an old and secret love, to which the countess has never confessed.' The clergyman only answered 'Hm, hm' as he filled his beaker and sipped from it with thoughtful mien. I had leaned right over the table on both arms the better to hear what they were saying. The cleric noticed

97

this. 'I think I may tell you,' he began again, 'that the two countesses have sent me to find out whether the bridegroom may not already be in these parts. A lady from Rome has written to say that he left there long ago.' When he mentioned the lady from Rome I blushed again. 'Does your reverence then know the bridegroom?' I said in some confusion. 'No,' answered the old gentleman, 'but he is said to be a gay young spark.' 'Oh, yes,' I said hastily, 'he is like a bird which flies out of every cage at the first chance and sings merrily as soon as he is free again.' 'And wanders abroad,' went on the old gentleman calmly, 'walks the streets at dead of night and sleeps on doorsteps.' This piqued me very much. 'Reverend sir,' I cried with some heat, 'you have been falsely informed. The bridegroom is a slim, morally impeccable and promising youth, who has lived the grand life in a castle in Italy, whose companions were countesses, famous artists and chambermaids, who manages his money very well—when he has any; who ...' 'Well, well, I had no notion that you knew him so well,' the clergyman interrupted me here and laughed so heartily that he turned quite blue in the face and the tears rolled down his eyes. 'I have heard, though,' put in the girl, 'that the bridegroom is a great and extremely well-to-do gentleman.' 'My goodness me, yes! Ah, what a mystery and confusion it is, to be sure!' cried the clergyman, still laughing so hard that he ended in a fit of coughing. When he had recovered himself slightly, he raised his tumbler and cried: 'Long live the happy couple!' I knew not what to make of this cleric and his chatter, but I was too ashamed of his story of Rome to admit to him in front of

98

so many people that I myself was the happy, if prodigal bridegroom.

The tumbler went the round once more, the reverend gentleman talking the while in the most friendly way, the general shyness dissolved and soon we were all in happy conversation. Even the students grew more and more talkative and described their travels in the mountains; finally they brought out their instruments and began to blow a jolly tune. The cool river air wafted through the branches of the bower, the evening sun was already gilding forest and valley as they rapidly glided past us, whilst the banks echoed to the sound of the French horn.

Our clerical friend was greatly charmed by the music and began telling gay stories of his youth: how he too had wandered over hill and dale during his vacations, how he had often been hungry and thirsty but always cheerful and how one's student years were indeed one long holiday between school, so cramped and gloomy, and the serious practice of a profession. At this the students drank another round and struck up a new song with such vigour that the mountains rang with the sound:

As southward birds are turning,
And all at once take flight,
The wanderers are burning
To stride through morning light.
The students yell with pleasure
And leave their hearths and home,
They play a farewell measure
For far they mean to roam.
Youthful voices gaily ringing,
To Prague a last farewell are singing.
Et habeat bonam pacem,
Qui sedet post fornacem!

99

As through bright windows glancing,
At night, in distant towns,
We watch fair ladies dancing
In soft and shing gowns,
We blow a tune of greeting
And earn a welcome thirst,
Let music mark this meeting,
But, host, some liquor first!
Soon our hearts are warm and glowing,
And free the wine is flowing.
Venit ex sua domo—
Beatus ille homo!

And when bare branches quiver
While Northern blasts blow cold,
In snow-lined fields we shiver—
Our shoes are torn and old,
Our shabby cloaks set flying,
We tramp through sodden lanes.
Some music—let's keep trying!
And the brave refrains:
Beatus ille homo,
Qui sedet in suo domo,
Et sedet post fornacem
Et habet bonam pacem!

The sailors, the girl and I, although none of us knew
any Latin, all joined in, shouting the chorus of each verse,
but it was I who carolled with the greatest gusto for I had
just espied in the distance my little toll-house and soon
afterwards in the evening sunlight I saw the castle
emerging through the trees.

10

—◦⟳⟳❀⁞⟋⟍⟀❀⟨⟨⟨◦—

The ship touched the bank, we sprang ashore and set off in our several directions through the greenwood like birds when the cage door is suddenly opened. The clerical gentleman bade us a hasty adieu and strode off towards the castle. The students, on the other hand, made for some secluded bushes where they set to beating the dust out of their cloaks, washed themselves in the neighbouring stream and started shaving one another. The new chambermaid finally made off with her canary and the bundle of clothes under her arm towards the inn at the foot of the castle hill in order to seek a room from the innkeeper's wife, whom I had recommended to her as a good hostess, where she might change into a better dress before presenting herself at the castle. The beauty of the evening raised my spirits and when all the others had hastened away I wasted little time in thought and at once ran off towards the castle garden.

My toll-keeper's house, which I had to pass, was still standing in its old spot, the tall trees from the estate garden still rustled above it and a yellow-hammer, who had always trilled his evening song at sunset in the chestnut tree outside my window, was singing still as though nothing in the world had happened since my departure.

The toll-house window was open and I ran joyfully towards it and put my head inside. No one was in, but the clock on the wall was still ticking calmly away, the desk stood by the window and the long pipe was in its corner as ever. I could not resist jumping in through the window and sat down at the desk in front of the great ledger. The sunlight fell golden-green through the chestnut branches on to the figures in the open book, the bees buzzed to and fro past the open window while the yellow-hammer sang merrily from the tree. Suddenly the door opened and a tall, elderly toll-keeper walked in, wearing my polka-dotted dressing gown. He stopped in the door at the unexpected sight of me. Not a little frightened by his appearance, I sprang up without a word and ran out of doors through the little garden, where I soon caught my foot in a vexatious potato plant which the old toll-keeper had, as I saw, planted on the porter's advice in place of my flowers. I could hear him running out of the door and cursing after me, but by then I was sitting high up on the garden wall and looking down into the castle garden with pounding heart.

All was sweet scent, glow of colour and rejoicing of birds; the lawns and pathways were empty, but the gilded treetops bowed to me in the evening breeze as if to bid me welcome and from the valley on one side came the flash of the Danube through the trees. All at once I heard someone singing from a little way off in the garden:

> Man's loud joy at last is still,
> Earth stirs gently as though dreaming,
> Leaves are sighing, moonlight gleaming,
> And the heart with secret skill

For old sadness now beats quicker,
Showers pass, dead moments flicker
Like the lightning on the hill!

The voice and the song sounded so wonderful and yet
so familiar, as though I had heard it once in a dream. For
a long while I pondered. 'It is Master Guido!' I finally
shouted, quickly swinging myself down into the garden
—it was the same song which he had sung that summer
evening on the balcony of that Italian tavern where I had
last seen him. He sang on and I leaped over hedge and
flowerbed towards the song, but as I passed between the
last few rosebushes I stopped at once as though bewitched. On the green lawn beside the swan's lake, in the
light of the evening sun, there on a stone bench sat my
gracious lady in a magnificent dress, a garland of white
and red roses in her black hair, her eyes downcast,
playing with her riding-switch, just as she had done in
the skiff when they had made me sing her the song of the
gracious lady. Opposite her sat another young lady,
whose white, rounded nape with its cascade of brown
curls was turned towards me as she sang to a guitar while
the swans slowly circled on the calm waters of the lake.
Suddenly my dear lady lifted her eyes and cried aloud
as she caught sight of me. The other turned so quickly
towards me that her curls swung over her face and when
she saw who I was broke out in a great laugh, jumped up
from the bench and clapped her hands three times. At
that moment a troop of little girls in short, snow-white
dresses with green and red ribbons came slipping through
the rose bushes, leaving me to wonder whence they had
come. Holding a long garland of flowers, they made a

circle round me, danced around me and sang as they danced:

> To you a maiden's wreath we bring
> With silks of lilac threaded,
> For you we lead the dance, we sing
> Young joys of those new-wedded.
> Greenest garland of the Spring,
> Silks with lilac threaded.

The song was from the *Freischütz*. I now recognized a few of the little songstresses, who were girls from the village. I pinched their cheeks and would have gladly escaped from the circle, but the pert little things would not let me out. Not knowing what this performance might mean, I stood there quite perplexed.

Suddenly a young man in gorgeous hunting habit stepped out from the bushes. I could hardly believe my eyes: it was the gay Master Leonhard! The little girls opened their circle and stood motionless on one little leg, as though bewitched, the other stretched out, holding the garland with both arms high over their heads. Then Master Leonhard grasped my gracious lady by the hand, led her towards me and said:

— 'Love—and on this all our sages agree—is one of the bravest qualities of the human heart. With one fiery glance it will shatter the bastions of rank and degree. For love the whole world is too small, eternity too short. Indeed, it is like a poet's mantle which every person gifted with imagination puts on in a cold world to make his journey to Arcadia. And the further away two parted lovers wander, the grander the billow of that shimmering mantle behind the traveller, the bolder and richer its pattern of folds, and that robe uniting the lovers grows to such lengths that others may scarcely walk abroad without treading on many such a train. Worthy master toll-keeper and bridegroom—although you, clad in this mantle of love, wandered as far as the banks of the Tiber, yet the little hand of your present bride was holding fast to the furthest hem of your train and dance, fiddle and intrigue as you might, you were drawn back into the silent spell of her beautiful eyes. And now that it has come to pass, draw the mantle about you, you two dear, dear foolish people and shut out the rest of the world—love each other like two doves and be happy!'

Master Leonhard had scarcely finished his graceful speech when the other young lady, who earlier had sung the song, approached me, laid a wreath of fresh myrtle on my head and as she set the wreath straight in my hair she sang in a teasing voice, her little face close to mine:

> Why am I with love still sighing?
> Why bring garlands for your hair?
> From your bow, the swift darts flying
> Find my heart and tremble there.

then stepped back a few paces.

'Do you recognize the two robbers who shook you down from the tree?' she said, dropping me a curtsey and looking at me with such a merry grace that my heart rejoiced. Then, without waiting for my reply, she walked round me. 'Yes, he's quite our old friend, without a trace of the Italian about him. But no—look at those bulging pockets!' She suddenly cried to my lady. 'Violin, change of linen, razor, travelling bag—all in disorder together!' She turned me round and round on all sides, quite unable to stop laughing. Meanwhile my gracious lady stood there quite still and unable to open her eyes for shyness and embarrassment. I had the feeling that she was secretly vexed at so much speech-making and joking. In the end the tears came welling from her eyes and she hid her face in the breast of the other lady, who at first looked astonished and then embraced her tenderly. I stood there in utter amazement, for the harder I looked at the unknown lady, the more clearly I recognized her as indeed none other than—the young artist Master Guido!

I did not know what to say and was just about to ask more questions when Master Leonhard stepped up and whispered something to her. 'Does he still not know?' I heard him ask. She shook her head. He pondered for a moment. 'No, no,' he said at last, 'he must be told everything at once, otherwise there will be nothing but more gossip and confusion.'

'Master toll-keeper', he turned to me, 'we have not much time now, but do me the favour of satisfying your curiosity here and now lest afterwards you aggravate people's curiosity with questions, surmise, invention and supposition!' With these words he drew me further into the bushes, whilst the other lady played with my lady's discarded riding-switch and shook her curls over her face behind which, however, I could see that she was blushing to her forehead. 'Well now,' said Master Leonhard, 'Miss Flora, who is pretending that she can hear nothing and knows nothing about the whole story, had given her heart to someone. There then came another who offered her *his* heart, with speeches, drums and trumpets, demanding her heart in return. But her heart was already given to someone, that someone's heart was hers and the someone did not wish to have his heart back, nor she hers. Everyone had joined in the argument—but have you never read a novel?' I denied it. 'Well, you have been taking part in one. In short—there was such confusion about the hearts that the *someone*—that is, myself—was obliged to take action. One warm summer night I swung myself on to my horse, put Miss Flora disguised as Master Guido on to another and off we set for the south in order to hide her in one of my remote castles in Italy until the uproar about the hearts had died down. On the way, however, they picked up our trail and Flora suddenly caught sight of our pursuers from the balcony of that Italian inn, in front of which you were keeping such a good watch—asleep.' 'You mean the hunch-backed signor?' 'Yes, he was a spy. We therefore withdrew secretly into the forest and let you drive on alone in the mail coach already ordered for us. This deceived our pursuers and what is more it deceived my people at the castle in the mountains, who were hourly expecting the disguised Flora and who, with more zeal than good sense, took you for the young lady. Even here at Vienna it was believed that Flora was living in the mountain-top castle, inquiries were made, a letter was written to her—did you not receive a note?' At these words I pulled the note from my pocket in a flash. 'Do you mean this letter?' 'It is addressed to me,' said Miss Flora, who until now had appeared to ignore our conversation, as she snatched the paper from my hand, read it and stuck it into her bosom. 'And now,' said Master Leonhard, 'we must hasten to the castle, where they are all waiting for us. And so finally, in conclusion, as is right and proper in every self-

respecting novel, revelation, repentance and reconcilia-
tion. We are all happily re-united and the wedding is to
be the day after tomorrow.'

As he spoke there emerged from the shrubbery a
spectacular rout of drums and trumpets, horns and trom-
bones; mortars were discharged amid shouts of hurrah!
The little girls began dancing again and from every bush
arose one head after another as though they were
sprouting from the ground. Amidst all the noise and
distraction I sprang hither and thither but it being
already dark it was only gradually that I recognized all
the old faces. The old gardener was playing the kettledrums, the students from Prague in their cloaks were
playing and beside them was the porter blowing away at
his bassoon like a madman. Seeing him there so unexpectedly I at once ran up to him and embraced him
heartily. This threw him quite off his stroke. 'Well, he may
have been to the end of the world and back, but he is as
much of a fool as ever!' he cried to the students and
puffed on in a fury.

In the meantime my gracious lady had slipped away
from this spectacle and flown like a startled hind over the
lawn into the depths of the garden. I caught sight of her
in time and ran after her with all speed. The musicians
were so busy that they did not notice us run away, but
thought that we had made our way to the castle, whither
the whole band now marched off with music and drums.

At almost the same moment she and I reached a
secluded summer-house with windows that opened to
look out over a broad, deep valley below. The sun had
long since set behind the hills and only the afterglow

shone like a faint red vapour in the warm, declining evening air and the rustling of the Danube's waters grew ever louder as the countryside fell gradually silent. I gazed steadily at the beautiful young countess as she stood before me flushed with running, so close that I could hear her very heart-beats. Finding myself suddenly alone with her, such was my respect that I did not know what to say. At last I found my courage, took her little white hand—and then she drew me to her and fell on my neck and I clasped her firmly in my two arms.

She quickly disengaged herself, however, and, somewhat abashed, she leaned out of the window to cool her glowing cheeks in the evening air. 'Ah,' I cried, 'my heart is near breaking with joy, but I can scarcely grasp it all, I feel as though I were dreaming!' 'So do I,' said my gracious lady. 'When I left Rome last summer with the countess,' she continued after a while, 'and we had found Miss Flora safe and happy and brought her back with us, but could find no trace of you, I never imagined that all this would come to pass. It was only today that the jockey, fast and fleet as he is, arrived breathless in the courtyard this afternoon and brought the news that you were coming with the posting-wherry.' She laughed softly to herself. 'Do you remember,' she said, 'when you last saw me on the balcony? It was a moment like this— just such a calm evening and music in the garden.' 'Who is it, though, who has died?' I quickly asked. 'Died— what can you mean?' said my fairest, looking at me in astonishment. 'Your grace's husband,' I replied, 'who was standing on the balcony with you that night.' She blushed deeply. 'What curious notions you have!' she cried. 'That was the countess's son, who had just returned from his travels and as he happened to arrive on my birthday he took me with him out on to the balcony that I might share in the shouts of hurrah. But is that why you ran away from here?' 'By heaven, indeed it was!' I exclaimed and slapped my brow with my hand. She only shook her head and laughed heartily.

I was so happy listening to her chatting to me so gaily and intimately, that I could have sat there till morning. In this mood of pleasure I pulled a handful of almonds out of my pocket which I had brought with me from Italy. She took some too and we sat together happily cracking nuts and gazing out into the silent landscape. 'Do you see,' she said after another pause, 'that little white mansion shining over there in the moonlight? The count has given it to us as a wedding present together with the gardens and vineyards, and we are to live there. He has long known that we loved each other and he feels deeply indebted to you, for had you not been with him when he abducted his love from her boarding-school, they would both have been discovered before she had had the opportunity of being reconciled with the countess and everything would have befallen otherwise.' 'Oh, my fairest, most gracious countess,' I exclaimed, 'your story is so full of unexpected surprises that my head is spinning. What about Master Leonhard?' 'Yes, yes,' she broke in, 'he called himself by that name in Italy; those are his estates over yonder and he is now to marry the daughter of our countess, the fair Flora. But why do you call me countess?' I stared at her. 'But I am no countess,' she went on, 'our gracious countess only took me in and brought me up in the castle because my uncle the porter brought me here as a poor little orphan child.'

At this I felt as if a stone had fallen from my heart. 'God bless the porter,' I exclaimed in delight, 'for being our uncle! I have always thought highly of him.' 'He thinks well of you too,' she replied, 'if only you would behave with a little more decorum, as he always says. You must dress more elegantly now.' 'Oh,' I cried joyfully, 'an English frock-coat, straw hat, breeches and spurs! And straightaway after the wedding we shall travel to Italy, to Rome, where the beautiful fountains play and take the Prague students with us—and the porter!' She smiled gently and the music played on from afar; in the still night air rockets flew up from the castle over the garden, from a distance came the rustle of the Danube waters and all, all was well!

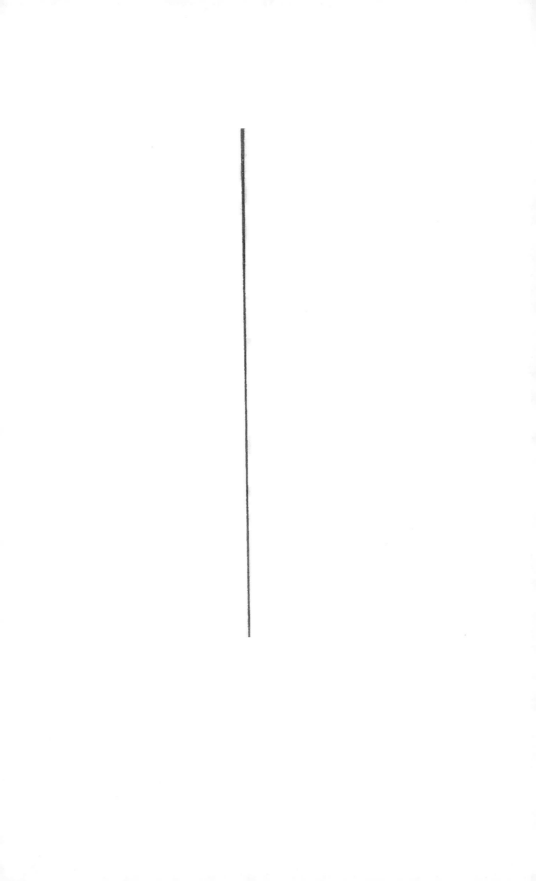

CPSIA information can be obtained
at www.ICGtesting.com
Printed in the USA
LVHW01s0020120718
583386LV00005B/158/P

9 781375 910712